2750:
LEGEND OF A LOCOMOTIVE

2750 taking water at Langley troughs

2750:
LEGEND OF A LOCOMOTIVE

HARRY WEBSTER

Illustrated by R. Barnard Way

ORIGINALLY PUBLISHED BY

THOMAS NELSON AND SONS LTD

LONDON EDINBURGH PARIS MELBOURNE

TORONTO AND NEW YORK

Originally published by :

THOMAS NELSON AND SONS LTD 1953

This edition 2016

Published by John Broadley

ISBN: 978-0-9507014-1-7

This edition printed by Dolman Scott Ltd
www.dolmanscott.co.uk

TO
A FINE TEAM

CONTENTS

FULL PAGE ILLUSTRATIONS

FOREWORD

THIS is the story of a pre-war locomotive and her top-link crew. In the pages which follow she has been given the number 2750. Railwaymen know locomotives chiefly by their numbers, and of those who read this book there may be some of riper years to whom 2750 will mean a lot – as much say as the names *Cutty Sark* or *Golden Miller* do to men in other spheres.

She belonged to that short but brilliant era of locomotive design which began in 1923 and lasted into the years of depression, an era in which our railways drew on themselves the attention and admiration of the whole world. It began with the amalgamation, on 1 January 1923, of 123 separate companies into the four great systems of London, Midland & Scottish ; London & North Eastern ; Great Western ; and Southern.

This gave such a stimulus and such an opportunity to inventive genius that a positive fury of creation, a sort of renaissance of locomotive engineering, followed ; and at the British Empire Exhibition at Wembley in 1924 the engineers of the rival groups put their masterpieces on show, side by side. From that moment the race was on.

The late Sir Nigel Gresley (then plain Mr H. N. Gresley) was Chief Mechanical Engineer of the London and North Eastern group, and his masterpiece was a three-cylinder Pacific with a boiler pressure of 180 lb. per square inch, and a tractive effort at 85 per cent boiler-pressure of 29,835 lb. This locomotive was the first Pacific since the Great Western's experimental *Great Bear* of 1908, and she might be called the progenitor of 2750, which followed six years later.

Though the persons and incidents in this book are fictitious, they are the sort of persons and incidents that were to be met with on the railways at that time. The book is true in the sense that *Hamlet* is true. As for 2750, she is intended to portray one of those creations of man which by a happy combination of design and workmanship and good fortune are so outstanding in performance and so sweet to handle that they become a legend. As *Cutty Sark* or *Flying Cloud* among ships, so ' Twenty-seven-Fifty ' among locomotives.

H.C.W.

Chapter I

THE NEW ENGINE COMES

NOBODY knew that the new engine, 2750, was coming down until Mr Smedley got a telegram about it from Doncaster Main Works. He was the District Locomotive Superintendent and he was sitting in his office with all the windows closed to keep the coal dust out. The mechanical coaling plant stood close by, and all day it kept hoisting wagons of coal up in the air, turning them over on their sides, and shooting the coal down into the bunker from which the locomotive tenders were filled. Every time the coal crashed down, a cloud of black dust rose up, so that there was always a haze hanging over that part of the depot. On windy days it was worse because then the fine ash blew about from the pits into which the fires from the engines were raked out when they had finished their day's work.

Mr Smedley sat at his table surrounded by charts and graphs and books. He also had a number of little bottles of oil in front of him, and on a stand at one side were various pieces of metal, fragments cut off from some part of an engine which had broken down - the leaf of a spring, a brass spindle about an inch long, a small piece of a wheel-tyre or rim, and so on. He was looking at some papers when a boy knocked and came in with a telegram. It said :

2750 LEAVING HERE LIGHT FOR YOURS 10.45 A.M. TODAY. NEW ENGINE. ALLOCATION YOUR DEPOT.

He let the boy go and pressed a button at the side of his table ; then read the message over again, looking pleased. There was another knock at the door. The man who came in was District Inspector Talbot.

' You rang for me, sir ? '

' Yes, Talbot. Look at that ! '

Talbot took the paper and made a little explosion with his breath.

' This is one of the new class ! Were you expecting her ? She's the first I've heard of so far south as this. I believe most of them are running up north and over the Border.'

' Well, I knew we'd be getting one or two additional units. We've *got* to have them to cover our summer service workings. But I didn't hope for one of the new A3's. They're a fine job from all I hear – and goodness knows we shall need some good stuff this summer. Some of the coast flyers will be loading up to well over five hundred tons. Further cuts on the running schedules too, if we're to hold our own against the other lines ! '

Talbot nodded. ' We can do with her all right. And she's coming just at the right time. We can get her run in comfortably before the new timetables begin. Who are you thinking of giving her to, sir ? '

' Who would you recommend, Talbot ? '

' Well now, that needs thinking about. She's a fine tool, and she should be taken care of. We've some good men here though, in the " top-link. " There's Williams running 'Forty-Six, and King on the Pullmans with 'Fifty-Four. Both of them are capable chaps, doing excellent work. Yet the man I'd pick for this prize isn't either of them.'

'What you mean is, you'd pick Eldridge ?'

'Why yes, sir, he is the man I had in mind. You think well of him too then ?'

'I do Talbot, although I don't often hear of him. Perhaps that's why. When I hear of enginemen it's generally because they've lost a bit of time somewhere ; run a big end hot or blown a fusible plug.'

'I'm sure he'd take care of her.'

'What's he running now ?'

''Seventy-Eight's his engine, but he doesn't get her as often as we'd like. To some extent he's an odd engine-man, and one of the things I like about him is that he'll do his level best with whatever we have to give him, rattletrap or greyhound.'

'Right ! Twenty-seven-Fifty's Eldridge's engine from the time she gets here, Talbot. When he comes on duty send him in to see me. Now what about running her in ? Careful's the word. She's brand new, down to the last bolt.'

'Well, sir, she's run up light, a matter of a hundred and fifty miles, which ought to help. I'd suggest two trips on the 5.10 Cambridge – plenty of stops and an easy schedule. I'll go with her myself on those two, tomorrow and Thursday. If she's all right she could go 6.5 a.m. Peterborough on Friday and Saturday. That's a bit heavier and a lot faster. Leave her in on Sunday for a look round, and let her take up her link position with Eldridge on the Monday. I believe he's on the 4.12 p.m. Grantham turn next week, which will be just about her mark.'

'All right then, Talbot, arrange it like that. You might let the foreman fitter and boilersmith know she's coming here for permanent allocation so they can get their record cards ready. And I'd like you to report to me when you get back after each of the Cambridge trips.'

'Very good, sir. I'll send Eldridge in. He's on duty at 3.10 this afternoon.'

With this Inspector Talbot left the office, and the head of Frederick Smedley bent again to his task. He was trying to think out a way by which the line on one of the graphs could be persuaded to stop climbing upwards and start sloping down.

A little before three that afternoon there was a knock on the door and Smedley cried, ' Come in. ' A wiry man with white hair stepped in and closed the door without hurry. It was main line express driver Robert Eldridge, a ' top-link ' driver. He was sixty-one, but he stood erect. His eyes were bright and alert, and he looked steadily and respectfully at his superior. He showed no sign of alarm. He was neat and clean, having just come on duty, but he was known to be a man who would be just as neat and almost as clean at the end of the day's work.

' Let me see, Eldridge, ' said the superintendent, after looking keenly at the other for a moment in silence, ' you're running 'Seventy-Eight at present, aren't you ? '

' Yes, sir, ' the driver had a deliberate way of speaking. ' I reckon her as mine, but of course I have to let her go a good deal just now. I realise that that can't be helped. '

' No, it can't. Trains must be run and if there's no other engine available, then yours has to go. '

' Yes, I appreciate that, sir. '

' All the same, Eldridge, you're doing some good

work on these important long-distance expresses. Your record for keeping schedule time ranks very high. Very high. And you've had some heavy loadings lately. The repair sheets show up 'Seventy-Eight as a well-cared-for engine, and I've never known you to be in collision with her or to let her get short of water. I know these things, you know, although you may not have been aware of it. I know them well. '

' Thank you, sir.'

' Now we've just had information that one of the new A3 class Pacifics is coming here new from Plant Works, number Twenty-seven-Fifty. It's the first one we've had, and none of us knows very much about the class except that the cylinders are slightly smaller at nineteen inches instead of twenty, and that they carry a boiler-pressure of two-twenty. I'm handing her over to you, Eldridge. She's your engine from now on.'

For a moment Eldridge was speechless. A steady, diligent man, accustomed to doing his best with whatever tool was given him, it had never entered his mind that he would be considered when there was something out of the common to hand out, far less that he should ask to be considered.

' Do you mean the new Pacific that's just come in, sir ? I saw her as I passed, and a picture she looked, too.'

' That's the one. She left Doncaster this morning – first of her type to come south. The finest thing in locomotives that has ever been at this depot. Perhaps the finest that has ever taken the road. You'll be the one to show us, Eldridge, as time goes on.'

' I hardly know what to say, sir. Of course I should take mighty good care of her. But there's Williams and King, both senior to me. I can't quite believe my luck.'

' It isn't altogether luck, Eldridge. As for Williams, he's running 'Forty-six, and King 'Fifty-four, and both are well-satisfied, I believe. And in any case I don't think they would grudge you your prize.' The superintendent smiled at the driver knowing him to be popular with his mates.

' Well, sir, ' Eldridge said, ' I can only say that I appreciate your booking her to me very much indeed, and I'll do my best for her always. And for you.' he added.

' Of course you will. Who knows but that the two of you may make history one of these days ? We shall see.' Smedley went on : ' I've instructed the duty list clerk to arrange for you to run her in. The program will be 5.10 a.m. Cambridge, Wednesday and Thursday. Inspector Talbot will go with you on both those trips, then 6.5 a.m. Peterborough, Friday and Saturday. We'll have a look round her here at the shed on Sunday, and if she is all right you can drop back into your link position with her next Monday. Where was she when you came in ? '

' On Number Six Road, sir, just outside the shed.' (Railwaymen always call a railway track a *road*.)

' Let's come and have a look at her, ' said the superintendent, reaching for his hat. ' Except I've seen the diagram and photographs, she's as new to me as she is to the rest of you.'

They left the office together and, crossing the coal roads, entered the machine shop, where the high-pitched note of carbide-tipped steel cutting into brass filled the air. It came from a lathe in the corner which was turning up a new connecting-rod small-end bush. Further along, another slower-moving and much larger lathe was reboring a driving axle-box. Under one of the windows on the left a planing machine was skimming true the flat surface of a crosshead-liner, while above all rose the high-pitched hum of electric motors and the singing of carborundum grinding wheels.

Smedley and Eldridge walked straight down the shop, past whitewashed connecting rods and side rods which men were examining to see if any cracks or flaws were beginning, and came out at the opposite end into the hot-water washing-out-plant house. This was whitewashed and spotlessly clean, containing two boilers and two large vertical tanks. The rams of Tangye pumps were clacking to and fro, driving water which was nearly boiling through pipes which led to the shed and finally reached No. 6 Road, one of the twelve 400-feet tracks which made up the Main Line Engine Shed. (The suburban engines had a shed of their own.)

At the outgoing end of this lay the new arrival, with a dozen or more enginemen, fitters, and rapt young engine cleaners grouped about her. As the newcomers approached, the crowd melted away, leaving only Talbot and the foreman fitter.

The day had been dry and there was not even a speck of mud on the engine. As Eldridge had said, she really did look a picture.

She was one of the new A3 or Super-Pacific Class, developed, after many trials, from the original Gresley Pacifics, As Mr Smedley had said, she had smaller cylinders but a boiler pressure of 220 lb. per square inch

A3 CLASS PACIFIC 2750.

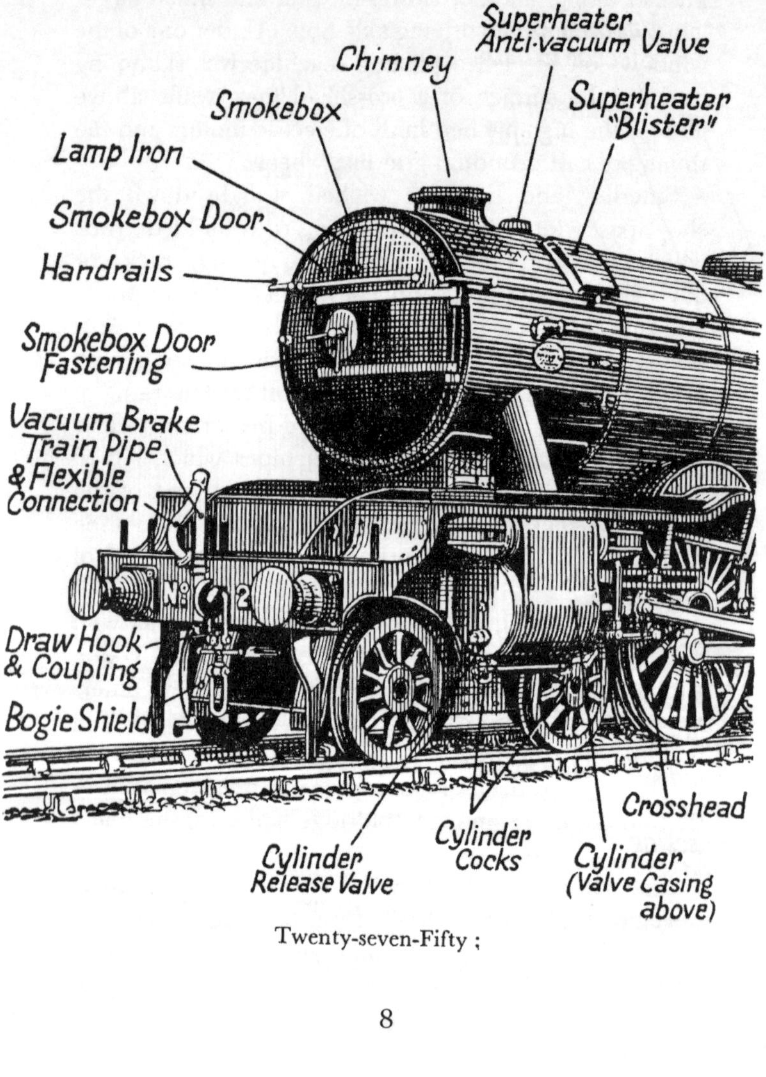

Twenty-seven-Fifty ;

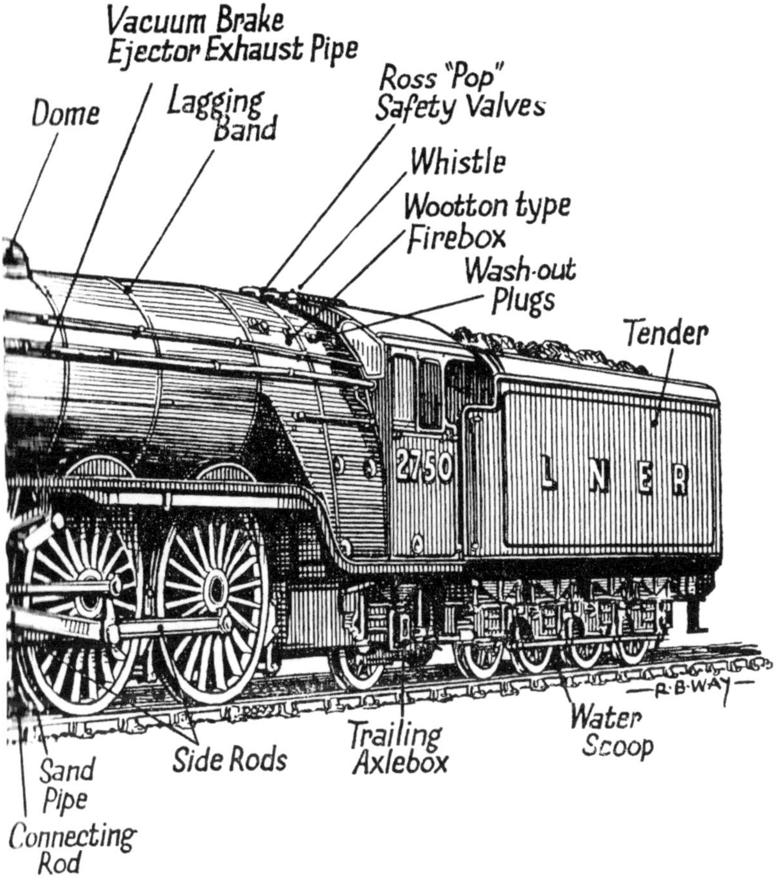

A3 Class Pacific

compared with the 180 lb. of the early Pacifics, and her *tractive effort* – her pulling power – was much greater.

There was one thing that marked her out at first sight as an A3, and that was the presence of two shallow oblong blisters, one on each side of the smokebox, lying a couple of feet or so behind the chimney and just beyond it. People, particularly women, used to wonder what these were.

' Isn't it lovely ! ' they would say of the engine. ' What are those flat bumps near the front for ? '

They were there because the superheater-header inside was so long that the ends of it stuck out beyond the circumference of the black smokebox.

In the grey light of a waning afternoon the new engine was an imposing sight. Her squat chimney and long, low smokebox were balanced over the bogie with so perfect a proportioning that more than one Royal Academician was inspired to transfer it to canvas. The long sleek line of her boiler was carried without a break up and over the firebox to the cab.

All too soon such grace of line and proportion were to be squashed into the unlovely, characterless, horizontal ' wedge ' – when the era of streamlining, ill-begotten of the Bugatti racing car, set in in this country in 1935. But there was no hint of that this afternoon – only a harmony of line and colour which filled the eye with joy.

Her long tapering boiler suggested power held in leash. On top lay a very low steam-dome, and a few inches in front of the cab weather-board there stood up two Ross ' pop ' safety valves, four inches diameter. Her six great driving wheels, 6 feet 8 inches high, were set a little forward, so that there was a very noticeable space between them and the pair of little pony wheels underneath the firebox. The gleaming lengths of steel which coupled the big wheels together and connected them with the pistons – the coupling rods and connecting rods – had ripple-like marks which caught and reflected the light. All had razor-like edges.

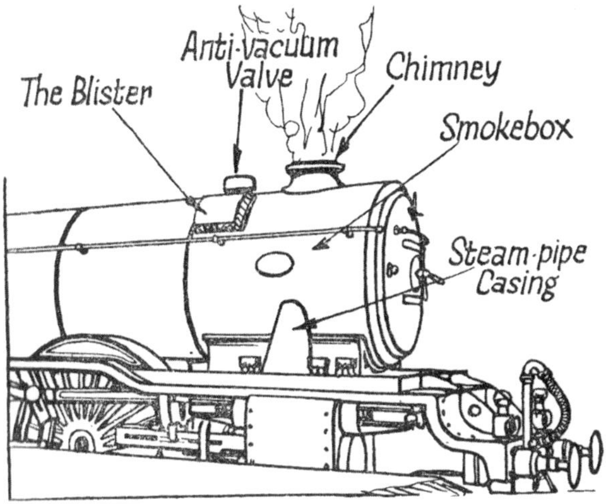

The tender was massive and plain, carried on four pairs of wheels spaced at equal distances. Tender and engine were painted apple green, picked out with black and white lines and varnished with copal. The smoke-box and chimney were black. Polished brass shone from the cab window-frames, from the splashers and the nameplates. Polished steel gleamed in the cranks and rods about the wheels and in the hand-rails along the boiler. Such was the A3 class Pacific No. 2750.

Thought by many and known by a few to have been the finest engine ever built at Doncaster Works !

Now the rest of this chapter is taken up with describing the mechanism of Twenty-seven-Fifty and how she worked. Those who want to get on with the story and those who are not very much at home with

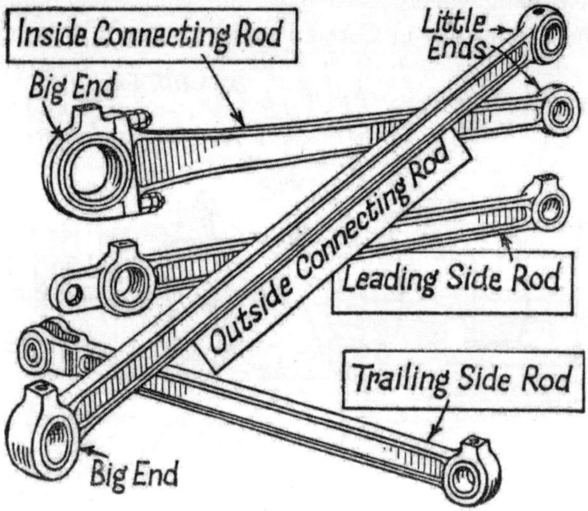

the language of engineers should skip this part and go on to Chapter II.

The others may care to know that 2750's cylinders were 19 inches in diameter, and that the piston stroke – that is the distance the piston travels – was 26 inches, as it was in the original Pacifics, the A1's. Her working boiler pressure was 220 lb per square inch. (If at this pressure, there were a hole in the top of the boiler as big as a small cigarette packet, and you tried to keep the steam in with your hand it would be like trying to hold a ton weight in that hand – apart, of course, from the scalding.) The engine had a tractive effort at 85 per cent boiler pressure of 32,909 lb.

The distance between the axle of the pony wheels and the axle of the rearmost driving wheels was 9½ feet. The pony wheels were 3 feet 8½ inches in diameter ; the driving wheels, as we have said, were 6 feet 8 inches. The former ran in Cartazzi axle-boxes, which let them

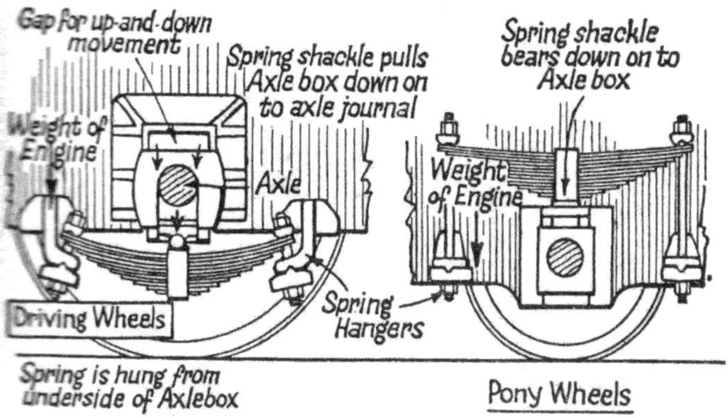

move 2½ inches from side to side, with the result that the locomotive went round curves very freely and easily.

The axles were all of forged steel, made under the Acid Open Hearth process. The middle one, shaped as in the sketch, was made up of five pieces. The machine-ground *journals* – that is the ends of the axles which take the weight of the engine – of the driving wheel axles, having to carry such an immense weight, were 9½ inches thick and 11 inches long. Each axle supported its share of the total weight independently, the bogie axles by helical springs, the others by laminated springs.

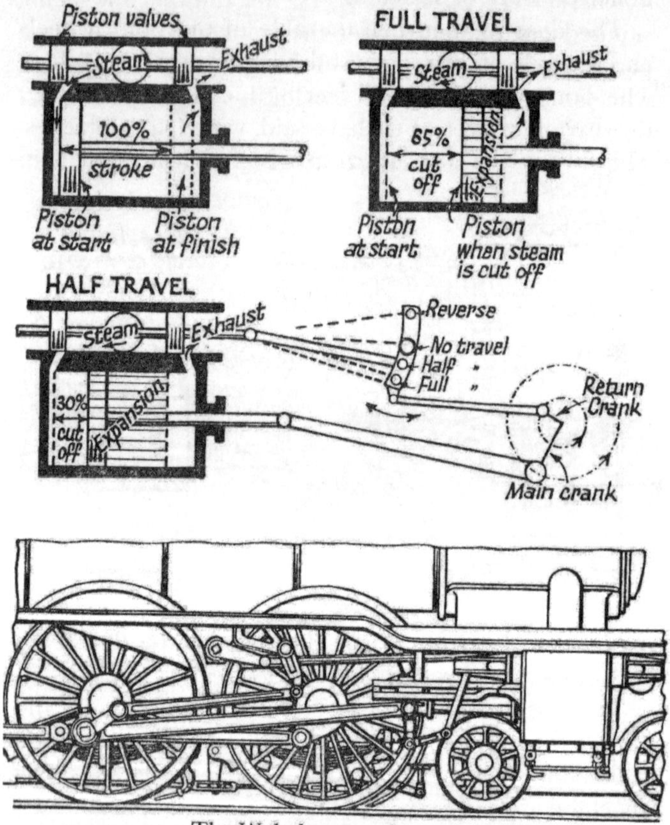

The Walschaerts valve gear

The connecting rods and the coupling rods were made of heat-treated nickel chrome steel, described as ' 50 tons per square inch tensile, ' and the ripple marks on them had been left by the milling-machine cutter.

There were three cylinders, the middle one being situated out of sight under the smoke-box. All three pistons were connected to the middle pair of driving wheels. Together the three cylinders developed 2,142

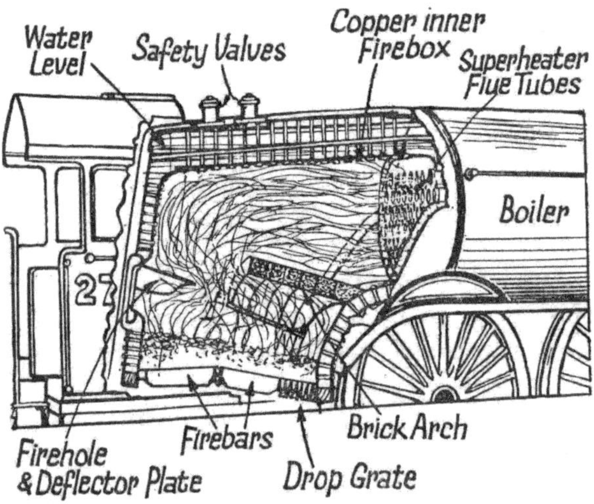

horse power. The middle connecting-rod was of the marine type, and the piston rods and heads, also of heat-treated nickel-chrome steel, were made in one piece, the former being hollow to reduce weight.

The valve-gear mechanism (the mechanism for admitting steam into the cylinders to drive the pistons and then exhausting it up the chimney when its work is done) was of the Walschaerts type, invented by the Belgian engineer Walschaerts. It was worked by that complicated tangle of rods and links outside the driving wheels which move about in such a fascinating way when the wheels begin to turn. But what interested engineers about the valve gear of the Gresley Pacific was the ingenious arrangement for admitting steam to the middle cylinder. In technical terms this is how it worked.

Steam generally was distributed through outside-admission piston valves, 8 inches in diameter. That for the inside cylinder was actuated indirectly by an arrangement of two horizontal rocking levers connected to the outside cylinder valve tail-rods. The longer of these levers had two arms, unequal in length, while the shorter was equally divided. Each of the levers was coupled at one end by its particular valve spindle by a short link. The long lever was pivoted on a fixed point and the short one pivoted on the short arm of the long. The opposite end of the short lever drove the valve spindle of the inside cylinder by means of a long link.

The cylinders and axle-boxes of the coupled wheels were lubricated by mechanically-forced feed, and oil pads were set under the journals of all wheels.

The automatic vacuum brake operated on the driving wheels of the engine and all the wheels of the tender.

The long boiler was a little more than 5 feet 9 inches in diameter at the front end where the barrel (the outside casing of which was, of course, green) joined the smoke-box (black on the outside). It increased to six feet five inches at the firebox (i.e. the furnace), which was of the wide Wootton type, with sides which sloped down and outwards to cover the full width of the main frames. In order to increase the heating surface and to permit the use of shorter tubes, the firebox proper was extended into the barrel to form a combustion

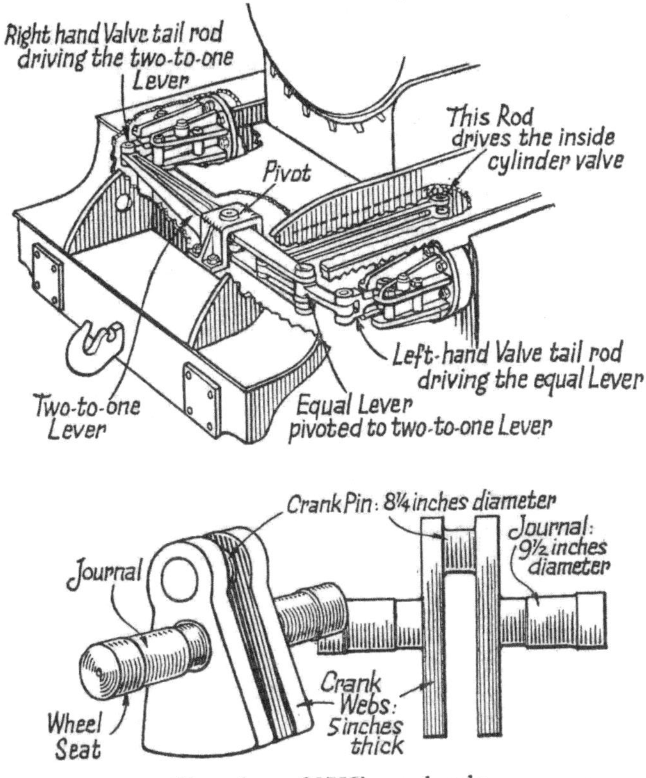

Two views of 2750's crank axle

chamber, an example of intricate boiler construction which roused widespread interest and praise among locomotive engineers.

The boiler itself contained 121 steel fire-tubes $2\frac{1}{4}$

inches diameter, and 43 superheater flue-tubes $5\frac{1}{4}$ inches diameter ; and the evaporative heating surface of tubes and firebox was 2,691 square feet. The dome enclosed a Lockyer balanced regulator-valve.

The bottom of the firebox sloped downwards so

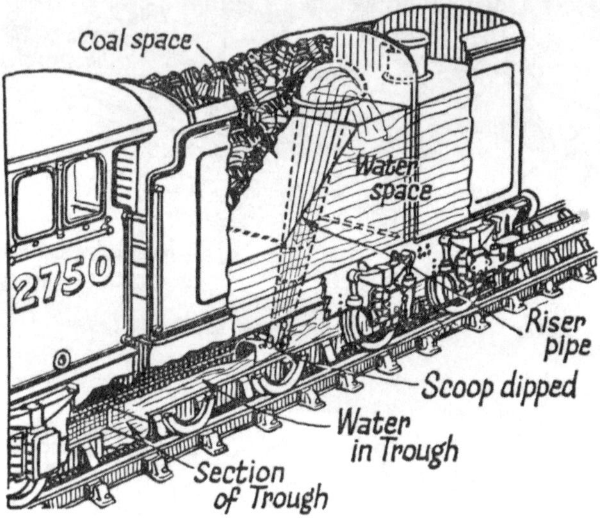

Exploded view of tender to show water pick up

that the coal was shaken well forward under the brick arch. The total area of the firegrate was $41\frac{1}{4}$ square feet. Twenty-seven-Fifty could burn up coal at the rate of 3,000 lb. an hour when it was necessary to do so, and her boiler of 1,749 horse power, except once only, was never known to be short of steam.

Her tender carried 5,000 gallons of water and 8 tons of coal. It was fitted with gear for scooping up water from troughs when she was travelling at speed, a perforated pipe-gauge showing the level of the water in the tank. The coal bunker was shaped in such a manner that the coal worked its own way down to the shovelling plate and the fireman did not have to climb up and rake it down.

From buffer-face to buffer-face Twenty-seven Fifty was 70 feet 5 inches, and weighed 154 tons 3 cwt.

CHAPTER II

WHAT CAN SHE DO ?

Long used to taking duty at all hours of the day or night, Inspector Talbot arrived at the shed on the following morning a quarter of an hour before the rostered signing-on time of the enginemen. But for all his punctuality, Driver Eldridge was there before him, and had already run his eye over the notices posted in the signing-on room, picking out and jotting down in his notebook those which concerned the running of his train, such as the relaying speed order at Knebworth and ' Short supply ' water notice referring to Hitchin Station down water-crane. It was not unlikely that he had been on the engine throughout most of the night – in imagination.

' 'Morning, Bob. You're early on the job this morning. Afraid somebody would run off with it before you got here ? '

Eldridge laughed. His fingers had itched to start on the work of getting the engine ready for her trial trip, but Inspector Talbot was riding with him and therefore in charge. Eldridge, well trained, would not do anything until his superior arrived.

' Know how the lubricators are set, sir ? '

' No. I'd like to look at them with you.'

' What will you put them at ? '

Talbot called over the fitter, who had been placed at their service.

' Full feed, both cylinder and axle-box, today and

tomorrow. A hot box costs more than an extra pint of oil. They'll be standard setting now, I expect. For the later trips you can drop to three-quarters. What's the setting ? ' he asked the fitter.

' Regulation two-fifths full feed.'

' As I thought,' remarked Talbot. ' Open them all out to full.'

This done, he charged both lubricators to capacity with superheater cylinder oil and top-grade express engine oil respectively, re-secured the container lids and, giving each wheel two or three spins to pump a supply into the oil pipe lines, descended from the footplate.

' Big ends next,' he said to Eldridge. Except for axle-boxes these are the most important of all the rotating bearings and the most likely to give trouble.

Eldridge unscrewed the top from that nearest to him with ring spanner and hammer, and Talbot drew out the looped-pin trimming from the stalk thus exposed.

' A Number Twelve,' he said, testing it with the special gauge carried in his waistcoat pocket. ' We'll have Fourteens in all the big ends and side-rods and go round them at Hatfield ; get us that far anyway. I'll take plenty of Thirteens, and if we're using too much we can slip them in there or at Hitchin.'

So were six side rod and six connecting rod oil-reservoirs dealt with, Inspector Talbot noting with approval the careful way each was charged with oil by Eldridge ; not the blind plunging of a grit-covered feeder spout into the open-ended stalk, but a steady flooding of the space around it until the level reached its top and clean surface oil flowed over and into it and down to the felt pad in contact with the bearing.

When all rod reservoirs were charged with oil and the screw tops firmly replaced, Eldridge went round with his feeder to those odd, half-concealed and generally

neglected oiling points, the lubrication of which contributed so much to his successful running. Along the top of the axle-boxes, coupled, bogie and pony alike, where the oil would find its way down between the horn cheek and the sliding face of the box ; under the footplate where inaccessible brake shaft brackets received little attention in the ordinary way ; in the oil holes and round the pins of the combination levers, union links and die blocks of the Walschaerts valve gears ; and a streak along piston rods, valve spindles and slide bars.

Lastly something important and special which Eldridge had found out for himself, and which was probably the secret of his success – a few turns on the cap of the grease cup that lubricates the fulcrum pin of the two-to-one lever in the Gresley conjugate gear. This is a point where but a sixty-fourth of an inch of wear is multiplied many times at the middle piston valve which controls the movements of the middle cylinder.

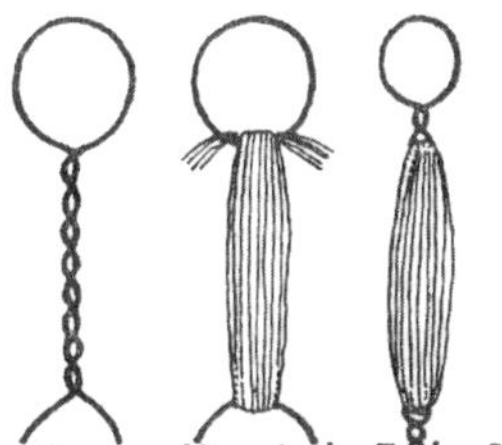

Lubricator trimming
(How to make one)

While the driver was occupied in this way, his fireman, John Clarke, appeared. He wasn't late. He was, in fact, a few minutes early, unintentionally. He was a little more than half the age of Eldridge, his ' mate,' and though a competent and trustworthy fireman, he had not Eldridge's attitude towards the new engine. To him, at thirty-three, a locomotive was still chiefly a machine by which one earned a living. It had to compete with other interests. He had had a long evening ; his head ached ; he was short of temper.

With a perfunctory greeting to the other two men he

went straight to the steps and climbed up into the cab, stowing his bright-green painted tin food-box, with its curved lid and little brass nameplate, in the tender tool-cupboard.

This done, his attention was turned to the ' front ' and he glanced first, not at the pressure-gauge, but at the level of water in the water-gauge glass, the most important of his responsibilities. For if it got too low, so that the fire reached the crown sheet of the firebox bared of water on the other side, irreparable damage might result or, at best, a fusible plug be melted out, the blackest mark that can be entered on the record of any engineman and the most dreaded by good firemen, among whom Clarke ranked high – and knew it. He found the level a little more than half-way up the glass. No outlet for his spleen there. He tested both water-gauges carefully, opening the bottom drain cock which emptied the glass and watching, as he closed it again to see that the water level, after oscillating up and down a little, returned to its original place. Then he turned his attention to the pressure-gauge with greater satisfaction to his present mood for, with forty-five minutes only before they were due off shed, it registered 20 lb. per square inch. This suited him much better, and leaning over the cab side he called to his driver : ' Twenty pounds is what we've got, mate. How do they think I'm going to get her up Stoke Bank with that ? '

' Well, we've got a bit of time yet, Jack.'

' Forty minutes, and I've got plenty to do in it without being firelighter for the whole shed. Lit up too late and looked at never at all.'

' Shove some on, Jack.'

' I'm going to. But it isn't my job at this time. I'll be putting on all I want when we get outside.'

Inspector Talbot interposed. He had been young himself and knew his man. 'Let's have a look, lad,' he said getting into the cab. He opened the firehole door, exposing the fire. It was spread evenly over the fire-grate and burning well, but a little thin. ' Lit *too early*, not too late, son, and getting thin. I'll take it up with the running foreman.'

He returned to Eldridge and Fireman Clarke began to feel better, his importance having received proper recognition. Several big lumps amongst the coal that he would have to break, provided occasion for further acrid observation. ' These new mechanical coaling plants want a stick of dynamite inside 'em. Never had lumps like that when they coaled us with tubs. Have to break 'em, I suppose, and might as well do it now as on the road and get my blinkin' head knocked off by an overline bridge.'

He climbed laboriously up on to the tender with his coal pick and proceeded with long, powerful blows to break the largest of the lumps. When he got back to the cab again he was feeling better still, the physical effort having released a little of his pent-up ill temper.

Sand boxes next. These should be, and had been, charged with clean, freshly-dried fine sand by ' sand fillers,' whose work it was to do this as engines passed through the disposal line when they came into the depot at the end of the day. But for some reason Clarke was never satisfied until he had lifted off the sand box lids and seen for himself that the work had been properly done. He had no particular reason for supposing that it had not been. It was just a habit that he had got into, a habit that was to stand him in good stead on more than one occasion. They were quite full and the sand pipes set fair to the rail so that the sand would drop on to it, and not fall wasted to one side or the other, and he returned to the footplate.

A glance again at the pressure-gauge, 60 lb. now. She'd just about do it ; nice to have a gauge with a dial clean enough to read, and this one was clean all right with its bright red line at the 220 lb. mark.

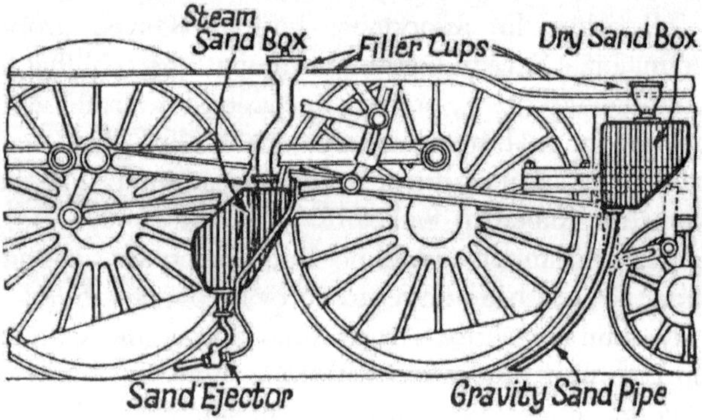

He wondered how long it would keep like that. Wondered too, whether she was a born steamer or a wet hulk like '93 and '46, both fair devils. You could put in as much coal as you liked and put it where you liked, but you couldn't hold the needle over. Back breakers ! '64 was another, especially with Tom Higgins cutting off at fifty all day long. This one might be all right. Cylinders were smaller. He'd get some idea after today. Humph ! A speed indicator too. Old Eldridge'll twist the needle of that round twice if he gets going down the bank, he thought. Clarke felt better. He got down from the cab and went to his mate, checking the tightness of nuts and taper pins under the watchful eye of Talbot. ‘ Keep the blower on, mate, I'm going for the headlamps. She'll have enough, I think.’

‘ Got a full set of tools ? ’

‘ No, short of a three-quarter-seven-eighth spanner, brush, and a few other things. I'll bring them.’ He went off, leaving a knowing grin on the faces of the two men.

‘ Good chap, Clarke,’ said his mate, and the other nodded.

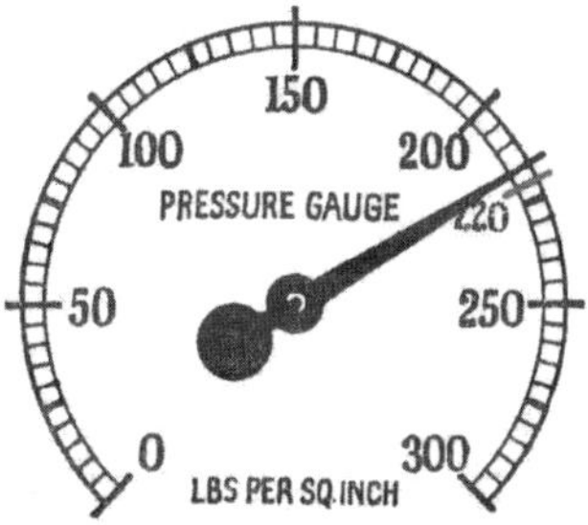

Boiler pressure gauge

When he got back, the engine had been moved out of the shed to one of the pits in front of it with the tender filling hole adjacent to a water crane ready for ‘topping up.’ Eldridge and Talbot were making a last careful inspection, looking for any trace of rubbing or chafing which, if not attended to, might give trouble on the road.

Setting the headlamps on the left and right outside lamp irons of the buffer beam, the correct code of identification for an express passenger train, Clarke again climbed up to the back of the tender where the water crane bag was handed up to him, inserted and held in the filling hole until the water began to overflow, and then thrown out. Back in the cab he tested both the injectors, operated when running by exhaust steam on his own side, by live steam on the driver's, and then turned his attention to the fire, adding a little coal over the thinner places and banking up along the firebox sides and under the firehole door.

After a few minutes he was joined by Talbot and Eldridge, who carried out a test of the vacuum automatic brake. Ordinarily this would be a matter of moments only and would consist merely of creating the correct 21 inches of vacuum and then, after closing both large and small ejector steam-valves, noting the time taken for the needle to fall back to the twelve-inch mark on the gauge. If this loss of vacuum occurred in less than thirty seconds it would indicate an excessive leak somewhere that would have to be located and rectified.

But in view of the engine being fresh from Plant Works, Inspector Talbot considered the more elaborate and severe ' leak gauge ' test desirable. This is carried out by means of a metal disc some four and a half inches in diameter in which are two holes respectively $\frac{3}{8}$ and $\frac{3}{16}$ of an inch, either of which may be covered or ' blinded ' by a moveable shutter. Removing the flexible hose pipe from its plug at the leading end, the disc is fitted over the opening with the large hole ' blind ' and the small ejector steam-valve opened to ' running position,' the test being that 21 inches of vacuum should be created and maintained against the leak of air into the train pipe through the small hole. The test of the large ejector is then carried out in a similar manner, but with the larger hole uncovered and the smaller ' blind.'

Through both of these tests the inspector was still not satisfied. It sometimes happens during the heavy repairs undertaken to a locomotive at Plant that a piece of paper, waste, or other foreign matter finds its way into the vacuum train-pipe, causing a partial blockage. In order to make quite sure that the vacuum pipe lines were clear on this occasion, he instructed Driver Eldridge to open the large ejector while the leading flexible pipe was still off its plug, himself watching the vacuum gauge to see whether, with the train-pipe full open to air in this manner, more than 5 inches of vacuum could be created. If so, it would reveal some obstruction that would have to be found and cleared. The needle fell to zero, however, and Inspector Talbot expressed himself as satisfied at last. There remained the sand gear to test, after which Eldridge drew out his watch.

' Four thirty-five,' he said, wiping his hands on his engine-cloth and glancing a question at Talbot. ' May as well drop down to the outlet signal. Always the chance of getting off the road at those facing points,' he added humorously. ' Had a rare do there Wednesday. The nine-twelve man managed to split them somehow and blocked the entire outlet ; regular bottle-neck that is. I reckon a depot the size of this ought to have an emergency outlet. One of these days there'll be a real jam.'

' Come with the other improvements they're talking about, perhaps.'

Eldridge touched the whistle, for it was not yet daylight, and men were busy about the yard. Clarke turned a wheel handle round to take the hand brake off the tender wheels. The driver carefully opened the regulator ; a cloud of steam rushed up from the front wheels ; and 2750 glided slowly forward. The signal light – the ' aspect ', as they called it – already showed green as they came up to it, so Twenty-seven-Fifty continued slowly through the points and into the mouth of Copenhagen Tunnel. Then she stopped and rolled gently back, tender first, past Belle Isle Box and into the gloom of Gas Works Tunnel, then out again and through the cross-over from down slow to down main, and on until she was alongside Platform No. 8, where Eldridge brought her to a stand with a slight *ring* as the buffers touched.

He was the driver who, years before, had bet his mates that he would crack a walnut between the buffers of his engine and those of the train and not destroy the kernel. They took him at his word, tying a nut to the face of a buffer, and in due course – ate the kernel.

Plenty of steam now, and at 5.10 exactly the train moved out.

The A3 class Pacifics were left-hand drive engines – an innovation on this line, on which right-hand drive had always been used as standard practice, a legacy from the roads. The change from right to left gave the driver a much better look-out for sighting signals and usually placed him on the platform side at stations, so that he could see the guard's ' right away ' signals more easily.

Consequently the reversing gear, or as the men called it, the ' lever ', was on the left-hand side of the cab also. (It was of the vertical screw type with a bar handle operating through ball bearings and with a power-locking device controlled by the vacuum maintained for the brake.)

According to the way Eldridge set this gear the engine would go backwards or forwards. But he used it for something else too.

When it was set as far as it would go in one direction, it admitted steam into each cylinder until the piston had travelled two-thirds of the length of the cylinder (that is, two-thirds of the way it had to travel) and then cut off the supply. It could be set so that the steam could be cut off when the piston had travelled only a quarter of the way, or a sixth, or even less.

To start the train moving after a stop the driver would set the gear almost at full. But when the engine had got up speed and was running along the level or down a slope, he would set the gear so that the steam was cut off much sooner.

It is like riding a bicycle. When you first start pedalling, or when you are climbing a stiff hill, you push the pedals hard all the way down. But when you get up speed along the flat, with a following wind, you press on the pedals only when they come to the top of their circle. Your foot really *pushes* only an inch or two then, though it travels all the way round with the pedal.

Engine drivers talk about driving with 50 per cent 'cut-off', of 40 per cent, or 30.

On 2750 full gear cut-off was at 65 per cent of the stroke, and it was Eldridge's custom to 'drive on the gear'. He liked to run with the regulator (or throttle) full open and obtain the draw-bar pull that he needed for any particular set of conditions by altering the point of cut-off. Thus with a light train on the level he might bring the lever up to cut-off at as low as 12 per cent of the stroke, with full regulator, or with a heavier train he might drop it to 35 or 40 per cent. When he was starting with a heavy train he would drop it as far as it would go – 65 per cent. This is the most economical way of driving a locomotive and easiest on the fireman, because it does not waste steam and so let the pressure drop. Clarke much appreciated it.

The regulator itself was balanced. To work it there was a bar fixed horizontally inside the cab running from the top of one front window or ' spectacle ' to the other, with a handle about a yard long at each end extending downwards, so that the regulator could be opened or closed from either side of the cab.

Clustered about this bar there were as many gauges as on the dashboard of a record-breaking racing car – gauges with faces like clock dials but (except for the one farthest left) only one pointer. The one farthest left was the vacuum-brake gauge, a duplex gauge, with one needle to mark the amount of vacuum carried in the main train brake pipe and another to show the amount of vacuum in the brake cylinders under the engine and coaches.

Moving right, the next was the steam-chest pressure-gauge, one of the most important and helpful for the proper handling of the controls, showing as it did the pressure of the steam just before it entered the cylinders.

Still farther to the right, over on the fireman's side, was the steam-pressure gauge proper, marked up to 275 lb. per square inch, but carrying a bright red line across the 220 lb. mark. This showed the pressure of steam in the boiler (always a little higher than that in the steam chest) ; and next to it was a Cambridge pyrometer, showing the temperature of the super-heated steam in the cylinder.

Still on the fireman's side and almost directly beneath the steam-pressure gauge was the steam-*heating* pressure-gauge. When the train was being heated this usually registered 60 lb. per square inch. Finally, under the fireman's seat, was the speed recorder, a complicated clockwork mechanism which not only showed the driver the speed of the train whenever he looked at the needle, but also marked it on a moving paper strip stretched between two spools so that at the end of a run there was a permanent record (rather like a barograph) for reference. This needle began to move rapidly round the dial in a clockwise direction as the train left the station, for the load was only 10 bogie coaches, a mere matter of 376 tons – little more than negligible to an engine of the power of 2750.

At Finsbury Park it had reached the 48 mph mark, and at Wood Green the 52 mark. At this point begins the eight-mile rise to Potter's Bar and Eldridge purposely let the needle slip back to 43 mph as they climbed it, his chief aim being to take things easy while running in new bearings and close-fitted sliding surfaces. Consequently they reached Hatfield two minutes late. This did not bother either driver or inspector. On the contrary, they delayed the train a further two minutes by going round and feeling the axle-boxes and connecting rod bearings to see if they had got too hot, each man taking one side of the engine.

All was satisfactory so far. So with a little more steam and a little less cut-off they got up to 62 mph through Welwyn Garden City, rising to 68 beyond Stevenage, and here Inspector Talbot thought it better to touch the shoulder of the driver.

' Ease her a bit, Bob.' And ' eased ' she was.

At Hitchin, two of the lost four minutes had been recovered and, with a booked stop of five minutes, there was time to see how the oil consumption was going.

All three connecting rod big end tops were the first

to come off, the most likely bearings to overheat under running-in conditions. The middle and right were well up in oil, but the left had almost emptied the container. Talbot quickly changed the pin trimming for one of slightly larger diameter whilst Eldridge replenished the reservoir. After the connecting rod small ends and side rod reservoirs had been inspected and one or two similar adjustments made the men returned to the footplate, feeling each wheel centre with the back of a hand as they passed.

' Left back coupled is a bit warm, Bob, but nothing to worry about. Just the pinch of a new boot. We'll have the keep drawn at Cambridge, though, before we come back.'

Four late again as the train left Hitchin, but Eldridge was growing less fearful of damage to his charge and once through the points at Cambridge Junction and on to the straight, he changed over to his normal method of driving – full regulator and early cut-off.

There was a roar as the regulator came back on to the ' Full ' quadrant stop, quietening as a few turns were given to the lever to bring the point of cut-off up – 35 per cent, 30 per cent, 25 per cent, 15 per cent. But the needle of the speed indicator was still moving over – 63 mph, 72 mph, 79 mph, 85 mph.

At 10 per cent cut-off the speed came under control at 88 mph, and Eldridge looked at his inspector.

' Won't do, Bob.' The latter said, 'that cut-off will run the big ends hot for sure. Too high a compression pressure on the pistons.' He smiled. ' Save it for the ten o'clock.'

Eldridge nodded, deeply gratified, and almost excited, for he had glimpsed the immense capabilities of this magnificent machine that was to be his own. He reset the regulator to the half-open position and dropped the lever down again to 25 per cent, which he found gave him a comfortably controlled speed, ranging between 60 and 70 mph. Thus through Letchworth, three minutes late, Royston one, to a stop at Cambridge, dead ' on time.'

Here 2750 was taken off the train and run into the locomotive depot for closer inspection and for turning round, bringing forward some coal, cleaning the fire and ' topping up ' the tender in readiness for the return run.

Again all oil cup tops were taken off and pin trimmings changed, this time for larger ones that would feed less oil to the bearings, but feed it for a longer time before emptying the reservoirs ; mechanical lubricators were recharged ; the keep was drawn from the left back coupled axle-box, examined and – the oiler pad being in order –replaced, all the connections in the oil supply pipe lines were gone over for incipient leakage and finally a tapping and testing of every accessible part for loose nuts, bolts or other fastenings. This done, one delighted and two well-satisfied men found comfortable seats in the cab, opened up their food boxes, and, at peace with the world, started eating.

The run back from Cambridge to London was in most ways a repetition of that down, except that Eldridge made no attempt to repeat his experiment of full regulator driving. Instead it was the turn of his fireman, Clarke, who being curious rather than anxious about the steaming capabilities of the new ' mount,' determined to find out. Saying nothing to anybody he contrived to keep almost a full glass of water when coming off the branch at

Cambridge Junction and, as the train left Hitchin, climbed ostentatiously up in the tender, seemingly to bring forward coal, actually to watch the pressure gauge and see how much of the three-and-a-half mile stretch of 1 in 200 up to Stevenage, would be accomplished without any further assistance from himself.

Not all of it was (for three hundred and seventy-six tons, though a light train for an A3, was still a load to reckon with), but sufficient of it to satisfy him. After the second mile the needle began to waver and at the third it had dropped to the 200 lb. mark.

Subconsciously Eldridge felt this and gave a turn to the lever, at the same time instinctively glancing up at the gauge. He turned towards Clarke. But Clarke had observed both movements and, tumbling out from the tender, swung open the firehole door with a practised hand. A few throws up into the front corners and the filling of a slight hollow arrested the fall of the needle and as the train passed over the summit of the bank at Stevenage and down the mile-and-a-half of 1 in 330 on the other side, a light ' pop ' from the rear safety valve told Clarke all he wanted to know. He lit a cigarette. Not a bad day after all.

A minute stolen at Hatfield to feel that left back coupled box, and a steady climb of the moderate rise beyond, brought the train to Potter's Bar on time and allowed a roll down the eight-mile stretch to Wood Green and an arrival at the terminus one minute before time.

Here they had a wait of twenty minutes until the coaches were cleared by an engine at the other end, then light to the shed for the final look round and the booking of any adjustments requiring attention by the mechanical staff.

' I'm going to report to the Chief, Bob,' said Talbot. ' He asked me to let him know how we got on. Book that box, and better have the brakes taken up a bit, the new pins will have pulled in now. I shan't come back. See you tomorrow.'

Eldridge raised his head from the bucket at which he was washing his hands. ' Tell him we've got the best thing that's come out of the works yet ! ' he called.

Talbot smiled. He'd picked the right man.

CHAPTER III

THE AMAZEMENT OF ANGUS MACKAY

So, by easy and carefully planned stages, Locomotive No.2750 was seasoned, and at length took up her part in the life and work of the depot.

She ran to Cambridge, then to Peterborough, then Grantham, Doncaster – farther and farther, faster and faster. *Yorkshire Pullman*, *Queen of Scots*, *Ten-ten*, *Four o'Clock* – all felt the pull of her drawbar as she roared North out of London in the sure hands of Driver Bob Eldridge and his fireman Jack Clarke.

Women set their clocks by her passing. Men and boys gathered – each at his favourite vantage point – to see her go through. Wood Green and Potter's Bar down platforms were best for a display of sheer pulling-power ; Hornsey up and Hitchin down for the thrill of speed, both points being usually approached and passed at well over 80 mph. Hatfield up platform to see the bogie pull her round that curve in heeling lurches ; Welwyn Viaduct for a sight to delight an artist, the spectacle of her symmetry and grace against the background of an English countryside. Farther afield one could stand on the little overline footbridge near Sandy and know the thrilling, frightening, experience of having her rush past apparently only an inch or so beneath. And on the up platform at Essendine one could watch and hear her stream down the bank and, whistle shrilling, flash by at 90.

All these places and others too were never without

groups of enthusiasts when the word went round : ‘ Twenty-seven-Fifty’s on ! ’

Important though they were, none of the trains she worked put any strain on her reserves of power. Sometimes a few extra coaches coupled on to cope with a rush of passengers would load her up to the 600-ton mark. But when Eldridge was told of it he would nod his head unconcernedly and drop the lever from around 30 per cent cut-off to around 40 per cent, while Clarke, having vented his spleen by cursing the idiocy of the travelling public in general and the passengers on this train in particular, would quicken his rate of firing from 50 lb. of coal per mile to perhaps 58 lb., and that was the end of the matter.

The driving technique of Eldridge varied according to the train he had. It was always full regulator in these days of crack train working, but according to his load, he would give and take so far as the booked schedule sectional times were concerned, keeping fairly close to them with light trains by maintaining uniform running uphill and downhill alike, but with heavier loads readily dropping two or perhaps more minutes on rising sections, recovering them by faster-than-schedule running on down grades. By this means he avoided anything that even resembled ‘ thrashing ’ his beloved engine.

Some trains were always heavy, often loading up to sixteen bogies, roughly 520 tons, and with these he would not attempt to cover the $17\frac{3}{4}$ miles to Hatfield in less than the even half hour, the booked time being 27 minutes. Eight of these minutes would be occupied to Finsbury Park, $2\frac{1}{2}$ miles, fourteen thence to Potter’s Bar, $10\frac{1}{4}$ miles, and the remaining eight from Potter’s Bar to

Hatfield, 5 miles. The first 12 miles out of King's Cross is very heavy pulling and by taking it steadily in this way when on the front of a heavy train, Eldridge avoided any disturbance of the fire-bed which might be caused by the powerful pull of the blast if he worked the engine with a late cut-off in order to get rapid acceleration up the 1 in 200 rise from Wood Green to Potter's Bar. Over the brow of this hill, however, he would let the train gather way and usually covered the 14¼ miles from Hatfield to Hitchin in fourteen minutes, regaining one of the three he had lost.

From Hitchin to Huntingdon, 26¾ miles, the running is predominantly downhill, and the train was allowed to continue to gather speed which at Huntingdon would have reached the neighbourhood of 75 miles an hour ; by covering that stretch in twenty-five minutes the remaining two of the three lost minutes were regained, 58¾ miles from King's Cross reeled off in sixty-nine minutes.

The skill and experience of Eldridge therefore left him with the considerable momentum of a 520-ton train travelling at 75 mph passing Huntingdon ' Right time.' And Huntingdon, when he was bound for York or Newcastle was, to Eldridge, near enough the start of his journey.

With such lighter trains as the Pullmans both *Yorkshire* and *Queen of Scots*, which seldom loaded to more than 400 tons, the running would be much closer to schedule, both uphill and down. With such loads Finsbury Park was usually passed in six-and-a-half minutes, Potter's Bar in nineteen-and-a-half, and Hatfield in twenty-six, an excess of one minute only over booked time, which was regained between Hitchin and Huntingdon.

With *The Queen of Scots* Up at Stoke Tunnel

This technique was repeated for the climb up Stoke Bank and the descent on the other side, whereafter the running was fairly level forward to Newcastle.

That part of the main line of the L & N E Railway which used to be the old Great Northern line is one of the finest in the country, and lends itself particularly to the kind of practical study which Driver Eldridge gave to it. Although he was probably unaware of it, it was his combination of road knowledge and driving ability which gave him the lead over so many of his comrades. Without the road knowledge he would still have been an exceptionally good driver ; with it, he was unequalled. It enabled him to get the best out of his engine in the way that the cox of a rowing eight uses his knowledge to get the best conditions for his crew.

The former Great Northern track was laid mostly with steel rails in 60-foot lengths weighing 95 lb. per yard. It has a ruling gradient of 1 in 200, but is steeper in parts. It begins with a quarter-mile level stretch from King's Cross to Gas Works Tunnel. In the tunnel it rises sharply with a gradient of 1 in 107 and keeps climbing past Belle Isle Box and through Copenhagen Tunnel, then levels out again.

Four-and-a-half miles out from London there begins the stiff climb to Potter's Bar, consisting of eight miles of 1 in 200. With Potter's Bar behind, the track runs down again but not steeply, then climbs, after Hatfield, to the famous Welwyn Viaduct with forty fine arches. Twenty-three-and-a-half miles out is Woolmer Green, the highest point in the first hundred miles. And a little beyond are the first water troughs, the Langley troughs, stretching for 594 yards and filled with treated water from the softening-plant on the down side of the line.

The track starts to slope down at Stevenage, and by the time trains pass through Three Counties Station and Arlesey, eight miles farther on, they have usually worked up a very high speed. We shall be travelling this road with Driver Eldridge more than once in later chapters, so there is no need to go over it now, mile by mile. Let us just mention Offord, a few miles south of Huntingdon. Here the line curves sharply first one way and then the other, so that there is a speed limit of 70 mph, which drivers dislike because it prevents them from getting a run at Stukeley Bank, a three-mile climb from Huntingdon Station to Leys Box of 1 in 200. Offord Curve ! Drivers do well to heed the yellow light there.

Let us mention also the drop down to Abbots Ripton Bank ; the speed limit of 20 mph over Nene Bridge ; the big New England locomotive depot near Peterborough ; the Werrington water troughs three miles beyond ; and the notorious Stoke Bank, the steepest and the longest slope on the whole line from King's Cross to Newcastle. Its summit, which is exactly 100 miles out, is 345 feet above sea level. For an engine with a load of more than 400 tons it is a gruelling climb, even though there are two short level stretches of three-quarters of a mile each on the way up.

There are two long stretches of 1 in 200, and 1 in 178, and altogether Stoke Bank means roughly 9 miles of heavy pulling after a preliminary 10 miles of gentler climbing. It is no wonder that many minutes have been lost in the ascent of it.

But many spectacular bursts of speed have been made by trains coming *down* it. It was the old 'galloping ground' of the Great Northern Railway, and the speeds attained there rose year by year as locomotives developed in design and construction until they culminated in the still unbroken record set up in 1938, when the A4 class Pacific No. 4468, *Mallard*, reached, and *held*, the phenomenal speed of 125 miles an hour – and momentarily touched 126 mph.

On the other side of Stoke Summit there is a long 22-mile slope, but as most trains have to pull up at Grantham on the way down (as it is the junction for Nottingham and Lincoln) not many speed records have been made there.

There are two more sets of water troughs before we come to the end of the old Great Northern line, one at Muskham, 123 miles out from London, and one at Scrooby, 146 miles out. At Retford trains have to slow down to 55 mph because the metals cross the old Great Central main line.

At Shaftholme Junction, 160¼ miles out, we pass onto what was the old North Eastern system, and now the line is remarkably flat. From Doncaster to York, 32 miles away, there is hardly a ripple, and beyond that there are stretches of absolutely level track, one 12 miles long. From York to Darlington the railway rises 175 feet, but takes 44 miles to do it in. And 220 miles from London, just past Northallerton, are the fifth and last set of water troughs, Wiske Moor. The track surmounts a slight hill between Darlington and Durham, with its peak at Bradbury ; dips down and climbs up again between Durham and the Tyne ; then crosses the King Edward Bridge to enter Newcastle Central Station.

The route from King's Cross to Newcastle is 268¼

miles, and Driver Eldridge knew every mile of it and drove according to his knowledge. Not everyone, however, understood his methods.

For example, one Angus MacKay, driver from over the Border, returning to Glasgow from London at the end of his annual leave. A short, quick-moving, perky little man who climbed up into the cab at King's Cross one morning a few minutes before departure time of the 10.5 *Scotsman* relief.

Planting himself in front of Eldridge, legs aggressively apart, he asserted defiantly : ' Mon, I'm comin' wi' ye as far as York.'

Clarke, leaning on his shovel, looked at him with a mixture of astonishment and curiosity. He glanced back at the platform clock ; calculated that he had ample time, if the need arose, to pick up this extraordinary creature by the coat collar and drop him into the ' six foot,' the space between the two running tracks, and then turned interestedly to watch the reaction of his driver. This was a welcome diversion that looked as if it might be entertaining.

But Eldridge was not entertained. ' Pass, please.'

Much to the surprise of both men Mr Angus MacKay produced with some importance the precious square of pink pasteboard that ' passed ' him from King's Cross to Glasgow ' on the footplate.'

Clarke thrust his shovel under the coal and disgustedly turned to his injectors. His life was made up of disappointments ; there was not going to be any violence after all.

Eldridge's manner changed. The man's presence on the footplate was quite in order and, that being so, he was perfectly ready to accept the newcomer in a good spirit. Cigarettes went round and explanations followed them.

'The week o' my life, mon ! Great Western, L.M.S., and now oor ain line, a' ower the place, miles and miles I've been, up and doon every day save yin when I'd to take ma wife to look at shops in Oxford Street an' sich places. Terrible waste o' time.'

'Do you mean to say that you've spent your week's holiday riding about on different engines ? '

'No' engines, mon. I could only get a pass for this yin. Just an ordinary passenger on they ithers.'

'What about your wife ? Help you check speeds ? '

'No, laddie, knitting jumpers most o' the time.'

'Some holiday for her ! ' put in Clarke.

'No' so bad as it may seem, son. We're auld-fashioned folk, and so we're happy ; the manner o't disna matter to either ower much. Last year it wis, and next year it will be, Craigendoran for her an' such womanlike gear as concerts and sailings. Efter that we reckon on a week at Ryde, Isle o' Wight. That'll be for me ; to see some o' they Atlantic liners, like the *Queen Mary* and *Empress of Britain*.'

Eldridge did not know quite what to make of this. On the one hand it sounded the oddest conceivable way of spending one's hard-earned holiday, but on the other he was intrigued by the enthusiasm of the man which in one direction at any rate – for locomotives – matched his own. Also it was clearly not the selfish arrangement it had at first appeared, but rather an ingenious way of providing two different forms of enjoyment.

'Why don't you let your wife go to Craigendoran while you traipse about the country in railway carriages ? ' Clarke asked.

MacKay looked at him as he would at a child who had asked a silly question. ‘ She wouldna’ go, nor I,’ he said simply.

Eldridge warmed towards this whimsical Scotsman. ‘ What trips have you made ? ’

MacKay’s enthusiasm lit up his face. ‘ Mon, we’ve got in some beauties. The best was on Tuesday when we came up on the Great Western’s *Cornish Riviera*, North Road, Plymouth to London non-stop all the way, two hundred and twenty-five miles. Ay, but that was a brave run. Some o’ those banks yon side of Newton Abbot near frighten ye. We’d one o’ the latest four-cylinder, six-coupled “ King ” class on, and a mighty job they are, four-cylinders, six-foot six-inch wheels and a boiler pressure of two hundred an’ fifty pounds, not a whistle less y’ ken. Divided drive they are, not like this yin, all the drive on one axle. Ay, a fine job ! Reached Paddington yin minute early ; giant o’ a run that, best I’ve ever had, and that’s a few. Day before we went doon via Bristol, yin of those two-hour expresses, 11 a.m. out ; a “ Castle ” on the front. That was a quick yin if ye like ; ye’ve to travel, mon, to cover one hundred and twenty miles in the even two hours, but we did it.’

‘ Where did you go on the L.M.S. ? ’

‘Doon wi’ the *Mancunian* ahint the *Royal Scot* herself, that was a rare trip tae. Came up wi’ yin of the “ Black Staniers ”. Pull onything onywhere, those engines, we could dae wi’ a few up round Auld Reekie. D’ye ken the type ? A Crewe and Derby product. Runs mostly in the Western and Midland Divisions. Only six-coupled and wee-like by the side o’ this yin, but like a wild cat when ye open the throttle. He must be a proud man to have his name hitched for evermore to such an engine as the " Stanier Black ".'

The slamming of doors brought Eldridge's head out of his window and the glance of Clarke to his pressure-gauge. Engineman born, MacKay stepped unasked

The 'Black Stanier'

into his position behind the driver, well clear of the arc swung by the blade of Clarke's shovel when he fired, and all three became tense for the ' Right away.'

It came very soon and 2750 entered the blackness of Gas Works Tunnel.

The speed indicator was novel to MacKay, and for the next three-and-a-quarter hours it was to be preferred to a gold watch in his pocket. His eyes seldom left it.

He had come prepared with a little notebook, in which were entered all the booked passing places and times in a neatly ruled column with another beside it for the ' actual ' times, and others for 'losses', 'gains' and 'remarks'. A stub of pencil was thrust under the rim of his cap. As the train climbed up through Harringay his interest sharpened. Unless he was very much mistaken this was going to be good. He listened and slowly nodded his head. Leaning towards Eldridge he shouted into his ear : ' Ye've a rare bit o' metal here,' he said. ' In three miles I ken it weel.'

' That's true,' replied Eldridge. ' But what makes you so sure ? '

' Her beat, mon. Listen to it, regular as a clock, the valves o' her were I ken set by a wizard ; chuck – chuck – chuck. Just listen to her, mon, 'tis music.'

Finsbury Park platform was reached as he finished speaking ; out came his watch and in went an entry to the little book. Not without a second look at the watch though, and a slightly puzzled frown on his cheerful round face. Down one minute on schedule !

He knew better than to comment at this stage. The loss might have been due to one of many reasons. That it might be deliberate, however, never for a moment entered his head. He kept his eyes on the speed indicator, his ears on the roaring exhaust – and waited.

The ascent to Potter's Bar occupied fourteen minutes, giving an average speed over the 10.2 miles of 43.7 mph, nor would the needle exceed it, and the frown deepened on MacKay's face.

He ventured a mild protest : ' Mon, she's a' but burstin' her boiler. Two hundred and fifteen pounds on the gauge ; only one hundred and seventy in the steam-chest. Could ye no' drop the lever just a wee ? We're actually losing time an' we havena' started yet ! '

' What were we late by the Bar ? '

' Two-and-a-hauf, ye ken. Ye're keepin' an awfu' lot up your sleeve and needna' ha' lost it.'

' See how we are at Hatfield.'

Hatfield was passed at 10.31½, the booked time being 10.29½.

' We're two late,' quoth MacKay censoriously.

' Ye've made up hauf a meenit,' he added, without enthusiasm.

' What does the fire look like to you ? '

MacKay took up the fireman's shovel, and with a practised hand used the blade of it as a screen against the fierce glare of the flames so that he could see the fire-bed. ''Tis a perfect fire, level and shallow, and 'twould ha' gi'en ye four meenits for the askin'.'

' Yes, but it wouldn't have looked as it does now ; I reckon a fire like that after our climb out of London is cheap at two minutes. Finsbury Park, Potter's Bar, Hatfield and the like, they're just so many trees, and if you look at them too closely you'll like as not miss the wood.'

' And whaur might the wood be ? '

' Newcastle.'

MacKay pondered this obstruse observation at length.

The train was now gathering speed, and at Hitchin the needle of the speed indicator passed the 70 mph line for the first time. MacKay's frown began to smooth out as he looked at his watch ; 10.44½, a minute recovered, one late still. Down the rest of the bank the speed continued to build up, touching a maximum of 84 mph at Arlesey, the bottom, and bringing the train to Huntingdon at 11.5, dead on time.

Which fact Driver MacKay connected with woods and trees and pondered, a process that kept him more or less silent until at Tallington he realised the growing nearness of Stoke Bank, and greatly daring : ‘ Mon, will ye gie us a run up Stoke ? ’

Eldridge turned. ‘ No need, we’re right time.’

‘ Och mon, I ken, but this isna’ an engine. It’s a meteor on wheels and I’ll never ride on the like o’t again. It wad be a grand feenish to ma week’s roving tae see whit this 2750 could dae. Mon, will ye no drop the lever a wee and gie us a run up Stoke ? ’

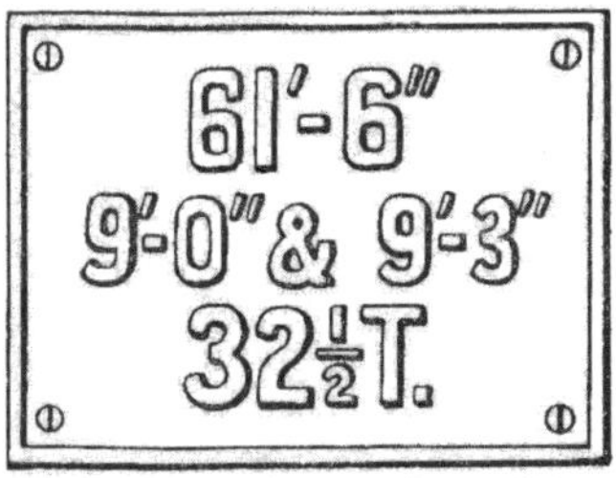

‘The wee plate at the end’

Eldridge found the enthusiasm of this little man from over the Border irresistible, and so, for that matter, did Clarke, who looked at his driver for a lead.

‘ You know what we’ve got on ? ’

‘ Ay, five hundred and forty tons. I took the weights of the coaches afore we started and added them up. They’re on wee plates at the ends ; weight, length and sich.’

This painstaking thoroughness turned the scales for him. Eldridge nodded slightly to his mate as he put a turn-and-a-half on the lever, dropping the cut-off from 34 to 38 per cent. 2750 responded with a surge forward and a deepened exhaust.

At Essendine, two more turns to 43 per cent, exhaust

a roar, and the indicator needle steady at 71 miles an hour. At Little Bytham it was back to 67 and thereafter the struggle was between it and Eldridge's lever. As the needle slipped back, another turn and yet another brought it up again. At Corby the engine was cutting-off at 52 per cent, but the needle had not fallen below 64 mph to the wondering amazement of MacKay, who watched the battle spellbound.

The last three miles to the summit were a losing fight, for there were limits to which Eldridge would go for the edification of his guest, but nevertheless Stoke Box, at the summit, was passed at a speed of 61.5 mph, probably for the first time in the history of the line.

'Losh me!' was all that the awed MacKay could say.

Nor had he much to add during the remainder of the journey to York, as 2750, running like a stag through the dales of the West Riding, covered the last 32 miles from Doncaster in twenty-eight minutes, cutting-off mostly at 15 per cent, and with boiler pressure never below 210 lb., to hold which Clarke was at pains to make it obvious that the firing of this engine was a mere flexing of the muscles between smokes.

Three minutes early in, MacKay got down from the footplate begrimed with oil and coal dust, but completely happy. He walked the length of the engine as if to satisfy himself that it was real and returned to say goodbye to Eldridge, who leaned from the side window of the cab.

'I'll no' forget much o' whit I've learned this day,' he said. 'Trees an' woods an' this miracle o' steel, Twenty-seven-fifty. I'm thanking ye noo. Goodbye.'

And his short stumpy legs trotted him off down the platform.

Eldridge's look followed him as he said to his mate : ' Odd little chap that, but you can't help liking him.'

Clarke grinned in agreement. ' Larning him ' had been rather fun.

CHAPTER IV

TRAPPED IN THE TUNNEL

THERE was not a great deal of 'double-heading' – that is, coupling two engines together to haul a heavy train – at the time 2750 was making history. The trend had been for several years to increase tractive effort so much that one engine alone would be capable of working any ordinary train over the main line. The two strongholds of double-heading, the old London and North Western Railway and the Midland, had both reduced the evil considerably with the advent of Whale's *Precursor* in 1904, and the Smith compounds in 1902. They stamped it out altogether when the *Royal Scot* of Sir Henry Fowler appeared in 1927, the first engine capable of taking 450 tons over Shap Summit unaided.

Sometimes, however, usually by an arrangement of Control, double-heading was still resorted to as the best way of transferring engines from one area or depot to another. It avoided recording in the books that an engine had travelled 'light' – i.e. by itself – and made the relation between coal-consumption and ton-miles look better in the depot statistics.

Such an occasion arose early in the summer season as the result of an exceptionally heavy week-end booking of passengers to seaside towns on the North-East coast. Some of the more popular expresses had had to be run in two parts, others in three.

As most of these extra trains were split up and the coaches coupled on to the ordinary South-bound trains for the return trip, some of the locomotives were stranded at northern depots with nothing to haul back.

So, Driver Eldridge was not surprised when, scarcely ten minutes before leaving York for London with the 2.22 p.m. up express, the Station Inspector came up to the footplate of his engine, already coupled to the train,

Double-heading on the L.M.S.

with the information : ' One of this type coming on in front of you.'

' How far ? ' said Eldridge, for to be the ' train engine ,' with a ' pilot ' attached in front is not very pleasant. He knew that he and Clarke would have to travel through beaten-down smoke from the leading engine ; that they would get only as much water from the troughs as the front man chose to leave for them ; that they would not be responsible for acting on signal aspects or for putting the brakes on ; that all they would see from start to finish would be the back plate of the tender in front, in short, that like a blinkered horse they would just pull and that was all.

'Through to London,' replied the inspector.

This simple statement was more than enough to set Clarke off. He lost no time in luridly describing to the astonished official exactly what he thought of the arrangement, of its instigators, of the Stationmaster, the Traffic Inspector, the District Superintendent, the General Manager and the Board of Directors.

To such length and detail that, while his castigation was yet at full tide, one of the early 180 lb. pressure Pacifics, No. 2561, backed slowly on to the front of 2750, and was coupled to her by the fireman.

In the general way when trains are double-headed, it is according to a plan of which both the drivers are aware beforehand, and they have thus an opportunity to meet and go over any point affecting their working ; such items as cut-off positions ; the length and whereabouts of relaying checks ; order of dipping water-scoops ; stopping position at stations, and so on. But on this occasion the instruction to work up No. 2561 attached to the 2.22 p.m. from York had been received too late for any such interchange of plans. The driver of the leading engine, one Jackson by name, did step back to the cab of 2750 and salute Eldridge with a wave of his hand, but there was no time for anything more, and he had scarcely returned to his own footplate before the ' right away ' signal was given and the train drew out of the platform.

The 2.22 p.m. was smartly timed, and on this occasion loaded to 510 tons ; it was booked to pass Doncaster at 2.58½ p.m., and it was here that Fireman

2561 passing upper quadrant signals

Clarke asked his driver about the matter of taking water at Scrooby trough, some ten miles on.

'Shall we dip first or last ?' he said.

'We've got no working arrangement,' replied Eldridge. 'He may leave us the first half or take that himself and leave us the second.'

'How shall I dip then ?' asked Clarke.

'Leave your scoop down from start to finish and we'll get what we can where we can.'

They approached Scrooby at good speed, and as the front man dipped his scoop Clarke did the same, keeping a sharp watch on the leading tender to spot when this should fill to overflow, so that he could judge the length of trough remaining for 2750.

The front lift-out was a bad one, misjudged and late, as was shown by the flood of water that streamed from the overflow pipe and ran off, full width, from the top of the tender in a deluge, carrying debris and lumps of coal with it.

'Greedy oaf !' was Clarke's laconic comment.

But sufficient was left for a full charge for 2750, and the train ran on towards the mouth of a tunnel, not a very long one as tunnels go, at 1,216 yards, but run through at speed by up trains, as it was on a short downward slope of 1 in 440. Retford, where the Great Northern and Great Central main lines cross on the level, lies about a quarter of a mile on the London side of the tunnel exit.

Near its entrance, Eldridge felt the brakes applied slightly by the driver on the pilot in front. This caused him no surprise, it being in accordance with the rules that the leading driver on a double-headed train controls its running, and he put it down to a proper caution on the part of Driver Jackson on account of the facing points and connections to be run through as the train emerged and approached the junction. Situated at the foot of the descent, these, he knew, could easily be taken at too high a speed.

At first, therefore, he took no particular notice of the check and eased back the regulator of 2750 in co-operation, but when the speed of the train fell first to 50 mph and then to 40, and still the brakes were applied, he bagan to feel surprise.

'What's he playing at ?' he growled to Clarke. 'We haven't so much time in hand that we can pull up for tea.'

'Reckon he's mistaken our booking,' replied Clarke. 'He's going to stop at Retford, and we're booked to pass it at three-thirteen-and-a-half.'

'Why didn't the fool check up with me before we started ?' answered Eldridge angrily and threw over the regulator again to full open. 'There was at any rate time enough to do that.'

The speed of the train as Eldridge spoke was now down to below 20 mph. It entered the mouth of the tunnel and 2750 began to roar as under full throttle she took up the load again ; a roar that to the astonishment of both Eldridge and Clarke was instantly echoed by another, equally powerful, from the chimney of the leading engine, 2561.

'He's opened up, too !' cried Eldridge in a voice of concern. 'Something's wrong !'

Still the brakes were on and the train slowing down, 10 mph now, not more.

Clarke thought he had got the answer, and shouted across the pandemonium which the exhausts from the two engines were making in the confined space of the tunnel : ‘ Somebody has pulled the communication cord ! ’

But Eldridge shook his head. ‘ Wouldn’t be that,’ he answered, ‘ the application is too powerful. The cord would only check us. We could overcome it with the large ejector, but we can’t overcome this. Whatever it is, it’s stopping us.’ He pointed to the duplex vacuum gauge. ‘ Look at that ! ’

Although both large and small vacuum ejector steam valves were full open and the double stream through the cones was sucking air, full bore, from the train pipe, the needle was visibly falling ; almost as he was speaking it dropped from five inches to two and as it passed over this mark to zero, the train stopped – as nearly as made no difference in the middle fifty yards of the tunnel.

The resulting silence, following so quickly on the deafening noise that had immediately preceded it, was quite uncanny, and this, added to their consciousness of utter helplessness, left Eldridge and Clarke looking at one another with an almost comical consternation. It did not paralyse them for long, however, and having stopped, clearly the first thing to be done was to start again.

To this end Eldridge promptly dropped the lever into full fore gear and opened the regulator, keeping his brake application lever in the ‘ Release ’ position. The engine gave a lurch forward, an ominous shudder, and then the coupled wheels spun round over a shower of sparks. They spun with a sickening clank of side rods and a dull continuous roar from the chimney.

Eldridge snapped shut the regulator.

Jackson, on the leading engine, tried next and managed to keep the regulator of 2561 open for appreciably longer than Eldridge had been able to do on 2750, but in the end the result was the same and the eerie silence fell again.

It was then that all four enginemen got their first breath of sulphur. It was not a very stinging breath, hardly more than the trace of an acrid smell and a slight tingling sensation in the lungs, but nevertheless – sulphur. In the case of 2750 the slipping had been prolonged, and had put a powerful draught on the fire, pulling its combustion gases through the tubes and ejecting them with the exhaust steam from the chimney directly on to the roof of the tunnel, whence they were thrown back downward into the engine cabs.

While disturbed, neither Eldridge nor his mate was anxious, except for the delay to the train ; and the latter pointed out that if the regulators of the two engines could be opened simultaneously, their combined effort might be sufficient to start. If this manoeuvre answered it would save the further delay that would be incurred in walking back the length of the train to release the brakes by hand.

' We might be able to do it,' he said, ' by using the engine whistles as a signal code.'

Eldridge touched the whistle of 2750 once, and Jackson appeared to get the idea, for he opened the regulator of 2561, but a little too quickly for Eldridge to be able to synchronise with him ; there was again the clang of violently shaken side rods and then silence. But this time with a difference, and that difference – sulphur – carrying with it the deadly poison of carbon monoxide.

Locomotive chimneys are never more than a few inches below tunnel roofs, and to expel from two of them, full bore, exhaust steam carrying a high sulphur content when neither is moving, results in a smothering poisonous cloud that is momentarily suffocating.

The passengers in the train were not affected. It was for them merely a matter for adverse comment and a closing of windows not already shut. But on the open footplates of the engines there began to come to the enginemen the realisation that their situation was more serious than had at first appeared.

Although breathing was still possible, the action was becoming painful. A definite effort was necessary to inhale, while each exhalation left a prickling in their lungs and, worse, the immediate need to inhale again. This would not have been alarming had the train been moving – but it was not.

The reaction of Fireman Clarke to the position in which he found himself was characteristically impetuous, an urge to get away from the footplate down on to the six-foot and make for the daylight on his legs as fast as they would carry him. Some indication of his intention must have been revealed by his movements, for Eldridge checked him.

' *Up !* not down, where it will be worse,' he said. ' Besides, if anything comes along on the down road or we get away ourselves, you'll be cut to pieces in the confusion before you can clear the smoke and steam.'

Clarke, naturally quick-witted, saw the reason in this advice, and abandoning his purpose stepped over to his coat and drew from the pocket a clean engine-cloth, which he folded in triangular-bandage fashion and tied over his mouth and nose, afterwards providing his mate with a similar crude, but not altogether ineffective gas mask. He then started towards the tender in order to climb on the coal as close up to the roof of the tunnel as he could, where a shallow stream of tolerably pure air still drifted. Before he could do so he stopped in surprise to see Driver Jackson from the leading engine swing round on to the footplate from the ' six-foot ' side. Not without a good deal of courage, he had scaled the coal on the tender of 2561 and dropped in complete darkness from the back handrail on to the front buffer beam of 2750. A miss would have thrown him through the space between the buffers on to the ballast, a fall of about twelve feet, where he would have lain unfound, for none of the men would have thought to look for him there.

Having landed on the beam, it was comparatively easy for him to step along the outside footplate, keeping good hold of the handrail, until he reached the cab and swung himself in.

' Something's got to be done, mate,' he said to Eldridge, ' and done quick. So I thought I'd better contact you because our only chance of ever getting this train out is for both of us to heave, and heave hard, at exactly the same time. We've got to drag her out by brute force, all wheels locked.'

He added that 2561 was carrying a full head of steam and noted with satisfaction that 2750 was also under full pressure.

The two men, both enginemen of long experience, agreed that the crux of the whole situation lay in effective sanding. If by its means the coupled wheels could be enabled to grip the rails, then the combined drawbar pull of two of the most powerful locomotives then built would, they thought, be sufficient to drag the train along, even with every wheel of it skidding, for it was too late now to think about releasing by hand the brake blocks that held them as though they had been welded solid to the bogie frames. Why they should be doing so, not one of the four men could understand, but that was now a matter of secondary importance. The immediate necessity was to get away from the sulphur.

They further agreed that Jackson, when he had returned to the footplate of 2561, should give a single short, sharp whistle to be the signal ' Open sand full bore.' Eldridge would give the second call after an interval of about ten seconds in order to allow the sand to drive well in between tyre and rail. This would be a double blast and would be followed immediately by the opening of both regulators steadily but continuously, full over to the quadrant stop ; the gears of both engines to be in ' full fore ' position.

If they moved no more than a foot, it would mean that the power effort was greater than the load resistance and therefore, however long it might take, the train would ultimately be got out. If, on the other hand, they did not move, even with such a power output, then, so far as the four enginemen were concerned, they might never get out. For they knew that the immense volume of steam that would be ejected from the chimneys of the two engines under such conditions, and in such a confined space, would assuredly carry with it poison enough to overcome them completely.

By now, breathing was both difficult and laboured, and it called for conscious effort. Any further carbon monoxide saturation of the atmosphere could not be endured ; the staking of everything was on the one chance that concerted action would move the train.

Jackson turned to leave, to get back on to his own footplate, moving as quickly as he dared, for seconds were beginning to count. Clarke accompanied him to the front of 2750 in order to help him climb the tender backplate, the object being to keep as high in the tunnel as possible. Shortly afterwards he rejoined Eldridge, and the two waited, somewhat grim-faced, for the code whistle.

It came – one short, sharp whistle !

Quite steadily, for to keep his head at this juncture was, he knew, the supremely important thing, Eldridge opened the steam valve of the wet-sand gear and listened to catch the faint hiss of driven sand ; then slowly and carefully he set his hands on the regulator handle, braced his leg muscles in readiness and nodded to Clarke to give the second signal.

It shrilled out – *Hoo ! Hoo !*

Now ! But to open even a Lockyer type double-beat, balanced regulator-valve against a full head of steam pressure requires an appreciable effort, and it was at just that moment that he was rocked and shaken by a rasping, tearing cough as sulphur-impregnated air struck his lungs. It brought his head down onto his chest and almost agony into his face, but it did not shift his hands from the regulator. With incredible endurance, twisting sideways with pain, he moved the lever over steadily, carefully and gradually, exactly as had been pre-arranged, until it came hard up against the quadrant stop at full open. Then his knees bent, his head came lower still and he crumpled up, an inert figure on the footboards. He was in his sixty-second year.

Had Jackson done as well ?

There was no sign of any movement of the engine, but then neither was there any sign of the dreaded clang of spinning side rods ; the sand was holding. It had now to be seen whether the steam pressure building up behind the pistons would reach a degree sufficient to push them forward and turn the wheels.

Fireman Clarke, when he had made his mate as comfortable as he could, went over to the cab window nearest to the tunnel wall and focused his eyes on a group of the bricks that lined it, lit up by the rays from the fire shining through the edges of the firehole door. Though almost imperceptibly, the bricks appeared to be sliding backwards towards the window frame.

The train was moving !

There was no apparent acceleration, but the group of bricks continued to slide slowly backwards until there came the bark of exhausted steam as the piston valve of 2561 moved over its port bar and opened direct communication between cylinder and chimney. It was followed by another bark from 2750.

This put still more poison into the air and caused Clarke to bring all his strength and will to the task of sucking in and gasping out the searing gas through his improvised filter. But there came also another twin bark from the two chimneys and definitely now the train was moving. It was announced clearly by the high-pitched screeching of the wheels throughout its length as they were dragged skidding along the rails. One yard ! Three ! Seven ! Ten ! And slowly the contaminated atmosphere was being left behind.

The steam-sands were still full open, and both regulators full throttle, exerting a combined drawbar pull on the train, even at an admission pressure of 85 per cent boiler pressure, of nearly 63,000 lb., probably the highest ever put on to a passenger train in this country.

Unable to resist, the train began to accelerate and the needle eye of daylight that represented the tunnel outlet and fresh air began to grow larger.

Breathing, though still painful, was more possible now, and as the two engines drew farther away from the fouled area, it became less and less a torture, until at length they broke out of the tunnel into God's sweet air and the sunlight.

Once clear of the mouth, both regulators and sand gears were shut, and regardless alike of time-table schedules and impatient passengers, the men relaxed into gasping, hiccoughing exhaustion.

Their first concern was for Eldridge, who had succumbed to the combination of physical effort and semi-suffocation. His need, however, like that of them all, was for breathable air, and with it now pouring into his lungs he quickly recovered and drank copiously of cold tea from his bottle. He was in no condition to handle 2750, but as the actual driving and signal reading would be done by Jackson on the leading engine, he expressed himself fit enough, with Clarke's aid, to get her home.

While he was resting, Jackson made an examination of both engines in an endeavour to find out what had occurred. With the vacuum ejector brake application handle up in the ' release ' position, he went round all the joints and connections of the brake pipe lines, listening for the rush of air into the system that would disclose to him the whereabouts of the leakage that had caused the brakes to come on.

His own engine was as tight as a drum everywhere, but when he came to 2750 there was no need to get underneath it, for the hiss of inrushing air could plainly be heard from where he stood in the six-foot. The brass cage containing the rubber ball that seals the open-ended drip pipe had been completely broken off, so that the ball had dropped clear, leaving uncovered the end of the $\frac{3}{4}$ inch extension piece leading directly into the main train-pipe that it should have sealed, and admitting air much faster than the ejectors on the engines could pull it out. This leak was equal to a full application from the footplate, and had brought the brake hard on.

Once traced, the fault was quickly remedied. Taking his mate's coal pick, Jackson deftly knocked a key from one of the sleepered chairs under one of the rails. Straight-grained, Burmese teak wood, this readily split. With a chisel he split off an inch and with his penknife roughly fashioned it to a finger, pointed at one end.

The hand-hammer next, and with both stuffed into his pocket, he crawled between the wheels until he was under the footplate and within reach of the open end of the extension-piece. Into this he pushed his home-made plug, driving it well up with a few smart blows with his hammer, closing it as effectively and tightly as the ball would have done. Flinging the hammer out he followed it in time to hear his effort rewarded by the metallic rustling sigh of brake rigging as, in pairs, the brake blocks dropped away from the wheels.

With a glance at his watch and an encouraging word to Eldridge as he passed, Jackson lost no more time.

He remounted the footplate of 2561 and, touching the whistle as a signal to the guard, opened the regulator, this time with instant effect on the train. The exhaust beats of 2750 followed in like an accompaniment, and the 2.22 p.m. up York continued on her way.

During most of the journey home, Driver Eldridge sat with his head out of the window breathing in the cool clean air, but he brought it in once to say something when the two engines cleared the next set of water troughs at Muskham.

' The next pilot that comes on in front of me is going to pull his scoop out of these troughs with two feet to spare in the tender.'

' Why ? '

Eldridge pointed to the water once again flooding down from the back of the leading tender, bringing with it as before, debris and coal.

' That's what did it. When he flushed the top of his tender at Scrooby he washed off half a ton of coal and a lump fell into the trough. We hit it with our own scoop and knocked it forward onto the ball cage, broke it off, let the ball drop and the air in, and on went the brakes. That fireman's clumsiness is what we've to thank for a pretty bad half hour.'

While he never regarded reasonable grounds as a necessary preliminary for quarrelling, Clarke nevertheless derived added satisfaction when they were presented to him ready-made, as it were ; they added the savour of justification to his anger like sauce to a steak, and it was therefore with ominous quiet that he remarked as he picked up his shovel again :

' Yes ! I'll mention it to him when we run in.'

CHAPTER V

NORTH WITH THE FLYING SCOTSMAN

DONCASTER, Leeds, York, Newcastle, Edinburgh. Farther and farther ; faster and faster.

Scarborough Flyer, Night Scotsman, Aberdonian, Norseman, Flying Scotsman – all came behind No. 2750 in their turn to speed northbound out of London over mile after mile of bright steel track.

Up hill, down hill, through tunnel and cutting, over embankment, bridge and viaduct, round curves, along the straight, clattering over crossings and rushing through stations, she ran them all, heavy and light, the length of England.

And she ran them to time.

But it was the *Flying Scotsman* that Eldridge liked best to have behind him ; notwithstanding his years and sobriety of character, he always had a feeling of intense pride, almost of elation, when he was running the famous *Ten o' Clock.*

Perhaps that was because he was then conscious of a sense of achievement, of having attained the goal of his life's work and reached the summit of his ambition.

Running freely down a bank, head a little out of his window, hand on the vacuum brake application handle, alert eyes watching the signals as they flicked by, sometimes his shoulders would lift and square a little and a look of deep satisfaction settle over his face. For at such times Driver Robert Eldridge was a very happy man. And certainly, from buffer to buffer, men, machine

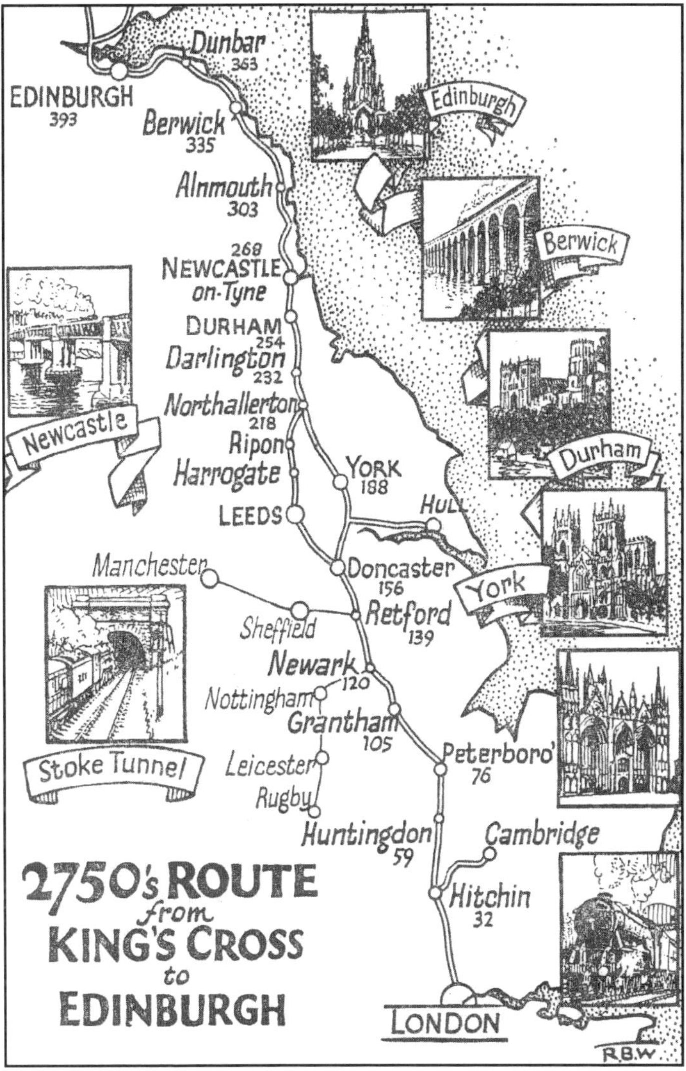
2750's ROUTE from KING'S CROSS to EDINBURGH
EDINBURGH
393
Dunbar
363
Berwick
335
Alnmouth
303
268
NEWCASTLE on-Tyne
DURHAM
254
Darlington
232
Northallerton
218
Ripon
Harrogate
LEEDS
YORK
188
HULL
Manchester
Doncaster
156
Sheffield
Retford
139
Newark
120
Nottingham
Grantham
105
Leicester
Rugby
Peterboro'
76
Huntingdon
59
Cambridge
Hitchin
32
LONDON
Edinburgh
Berwick
Durham
York
Newcastle
Stoke Tunnel
R.B.W.

and rolling stock were matter for pride, probably at that time the finest turn-out of its kind in the world.

The *Flying Scotsman* was the first of all trains to bear a name, but it is not known exactly when it was adopted. Before 1862, the morning express left London at 9.0 a.m. for Edinburgh via Spalding and Lincoln, occupying ten-and-a-half hours on the journey of 402 miles, and carrying first and second-class passengers only. Two years after the East Coast Joint Stock working was begun in 1860 the departure time was changed to 10.0 a.m. and, except for a short period of dislocation during the war of 1914-18, has remained unaltered.

In 1862 the journey was accomplished in ten-and-a-half hours, in 1872 in nine-and-a-half hours, in 1876 in nine hours, in 1888 in eight-and-a-half hours, and in 1901 in eight-and-a-quarter hours. The year 1928 was that in which the *Flying Scotsman* first ran without a stop between London and Edinburgh, covering the 392¾ miles in seven-and-a-half hours, this time being later cut to seven hours. Throughout its long life the train has never been involved in any serious mishap.

Only locomotives in the very highest mechanical condition are ever set to work the *Ten o' Clock*, and always a 'pilot' engine stands ready to take over should one of them fail.

The rolling stock is of special construction, incorporating all such modern developments as air-conditioning, acoustic blanketing, vita-glass windows, electric kitchens and cocktail bar.

As the train loads normally to fourteen or fifteen coaches, in the neighbourhood of 550 tons empty weight, there was good reason for Driver Eldridge to be a proud man when he took the *Flying Scotsman* out of King's Cross.

Let us go back and watch him on one of those proud days. He takes his engine, prepared with special care, off shed at 9.30 a.m. according to his own huge-dialled silver watch, regardless of what the Greenwich-controlled clock of the depot may say, and, dropping down into the mouth of Copenhagen, waits for the ' set back ' signal. This soon lets him through and he passes, tender first, past Belle Isle Box, through Gas Works Tunnel, and on to the train standing at Number 10 Platform, the entire length of which it takes up.

No walnut-cracking approach on these occasions, for he is buck-eye coupled and must hit up and compress the buffers to make sure that the jaws of coach and engine coupling snap together. He will step down from the footplate and walk back to satisfy himself that he is properly coupled, and that the brake pipes are connected, then forward for a last look round the rods and the motion before returning, leisurely wiping his hands on an engine cloth, to the footplate. He will test his brake by putting the vacuum brake application handle into the ' release ' position, and watching the needle of the gauge as it rises to twenty-one inches, the releasing limit. This vacuum obtained, he will make sure that he can hold it with the handle in ' running ' position, which he will not always be able to do, for it does seem that if anything is to go wrong at the last minute it will be with the brake system. A badly coupled connection somewhere in the train, a piece of grit on the plug runner washer, a pipe joint that is tight, yet not quite tight enough – any of these will slowly drag the needle back and defy detection by fuming traffic officials and despairing carriage examiners.

But it will be detected in the end and quickly put right, leaving still time for Eldridge to lean from his window in the interval before starting, an interested spectator of the rush and bustle and last-minute admonitions of the crowd on the platform.

Fireman Clarke will be busier, principally with his efforts to keep the needle of the pressure-gauge just short of the 220-mark, and so avoid a minor explosion at the safety-valves. He will be working the damper to increase or reduce the amount of air passing through the fire, and adjusting the steam blower which controls the draught on the fire. If he cannot keep the needle down by these means he will have recourse to the injector and force cold water into the boiler – a certain way of reducing the pressure.

Clarke will also be breaking up odd lumps of coal to double-fist size, the best for firing, and swilling the footboard down afterwards with his slacker-pipe, to lay the dust. But both he and Eldridge will so contrive matters that during the last two or three minutes they are left free to look out for platform signals or any unexpected incident.

Clustering round the engine will be the ‘ fans ’ four or five schoolboys busily jotting down numbers and other details in little note books. One of the more daring boys will usually hold his book up for Eldridge to autograph – ‘ The Driver of the *Flying Scotsman*, most famous train in the world.’

At the minute to ten o’clock the big safety valves will prove the master of Fireman Clarke in spite of all the measures he has taken. They will stutter – if he is lucky. If he is unlucky they will pop into a roar of escaping steam. But it is too late to bother any more now. Whistles are blowing and doors are slamming. Eldridge's hand reaches back for the regulator handle ; then his head disappears from the window. The ' Right away ' signal has been given and acknowledged. He gives the regulator handle only a slight tug forward. The train is heavy and this would be the worst possible place to slip. There are so many points worked by

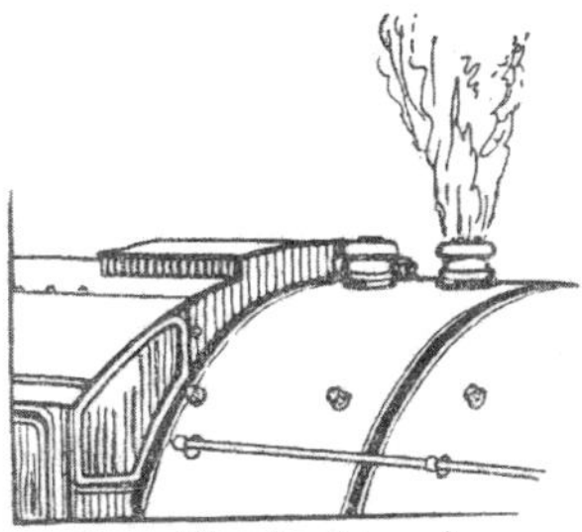

Ross ' Pop ' safety valves

electricity hereabouts that sand is not allowed to be used. The slight tug, though it does no more than lift the regulator valve off its seat, sends a rush of steam from the open waste water-cocks of the cylinders. The great locomotive gives a slight lurch forward, then the exhaust utters its first peremptory explosive bark. Other barks follow at rapidly decreasing intervals, as is the way with 3-cylinder engines, and the train draws slowly out from the platform.

Eldridge's head for a moment reappears at his window to look along the length of the train and see that it is all in one piece. He has to be sure of that, and he

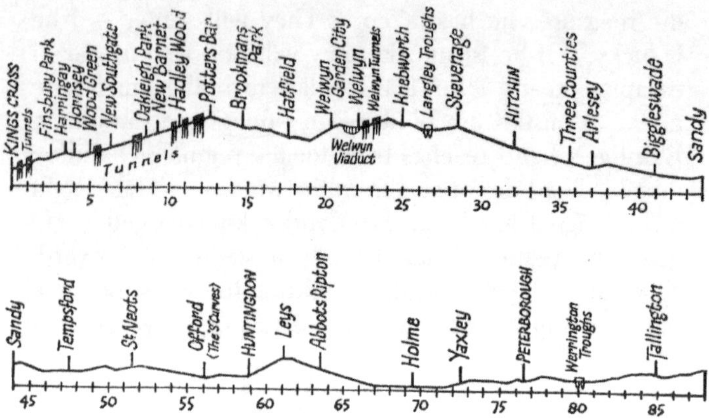

has to see that no doors are left open. Then the barks suddenly change to thunder-claps, and daylight changes to darkness. The train is in Gas Works Tunnel !

A glance at Clarke is signal enough for him to stoop down and close the waste water cocks. Cylinder and superheater elements alike are well clear of water now, and in a minute or two there is a further tug on the regulator.

Too much – or too suddenly ! The staccato barks change instantly to a continuous and deafening roar as the engine ' picks up ' the wheels and sends them spinning round. The constant dripping of slimy water from the tunnel roof onto rails makes them perpetually greasy. Eldridge will snap shut the regulator ; and when he has done so, but not before (lest the jar of too sudden a recovered grip bends a coupling rod), Clarke will open the steam sanding-gear.

The slipping stops, but the train has lost way. Moreover it is climbing the 1 in 107 grade through the

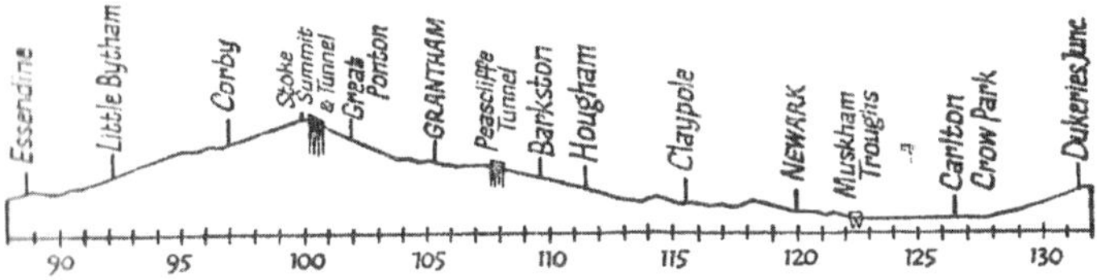

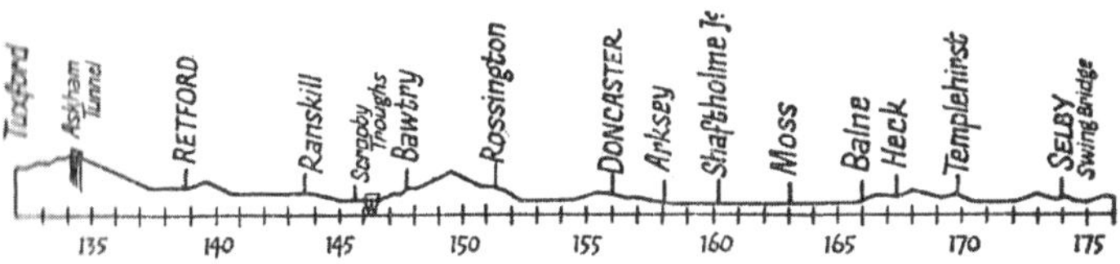

tunnel so that, although the steam-sand continues to run, the result of a re-opening of the regulator would be more slipping and a further loss of way.

Eldridge, showing neither concern nor annoyance, but with the patience with which he would treat a wayward child, tries again and yet again until in her own good time 2750 resumes her staccato barking and the train begins to recover speed.

Breaking out from Gas Works Tunnel into a burst of sunshine she passes Belle Isle Box. Then darkness again for the 594 yards of Copenhagen Tunnel.

No slipping here, but not until he comes out does Eldridge give the engine more steam, and then he offsets the effect of it to a large extent by taking up the lever to 40 per cent cut-off. The needle of the pressure-gauge will mark the increased demand for steam and flutter back to the 190 line, not unnoticed by Clarke, now at his best as a locomotive fireman, alert, active and proficient. With the blade of his shovel he trips open the firehole

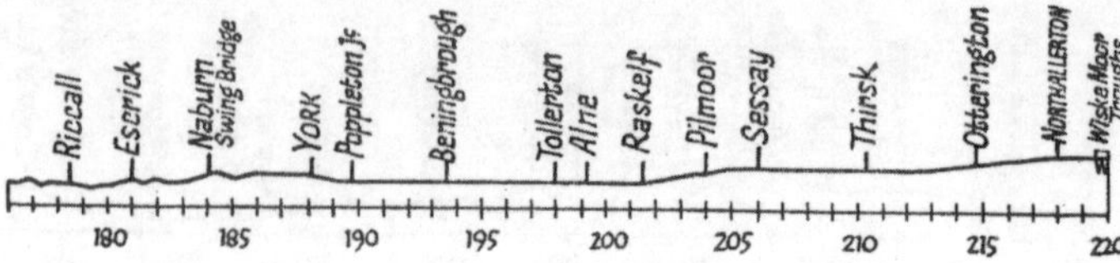

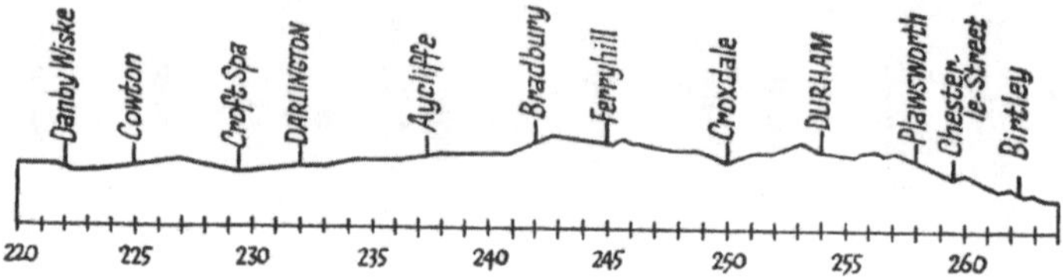

door and carefully places well-broken coal at the two back corners of the fire grate and under the firehole.

Within minutes the needle stops and moves back, up to 220, causing a slight pop of the safety-valves. The exhaust injector is already at work and will continue to be, probably until Newcastle is reached. Clarke opens the steam valve of the other and the popping stops. This in its turn does not escape Eldridge, who gives the engine more regulator still. Thus are supply and demand related by the perfect team-work of the two men.

Cutting-off at 35 per cent, the *chuff-chuff-chuffs* of the exhaust begin to merge into one continuous roar as the train passes the great London freight termini of Ferme Park Departure and East Goods Arrival, where busy little 0-6-0 tank-engines are pushing and pulling the wagons about the sidings. Then Finsbury Park, first sectional timing-point out.

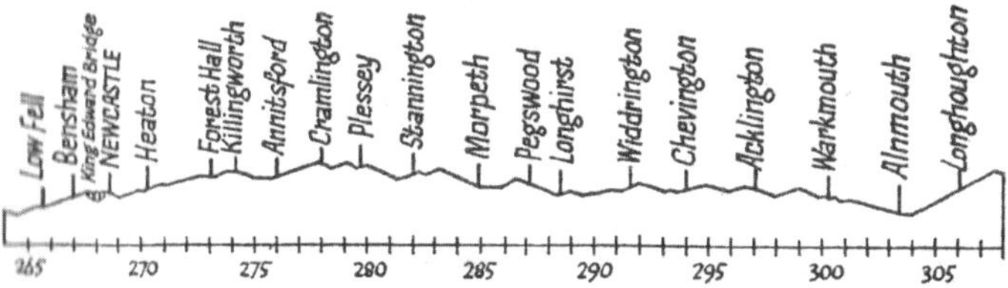

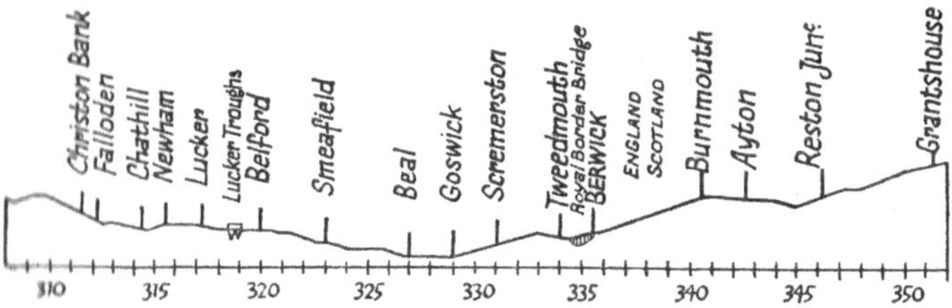

Eldridge consults his watch, 10.9 a.m. – too long in that section. The slipping in Gas Works Tunnel has cost at least one, and probably nearly two, minutes. While he expects to be late past Finsbury, it should not be quite so much, and with a glance at the pressure-gauge, he jerks open the regulator a little more still. On the easy running through Hornsey to Wood Green the train begins to gather speed and the station is passed with the speed indicator registering 51 mph. Ordinarily Eldridge would be satisfied and leave the cut-off unaltered for the following ascent at 1 in 200 to Potter's Bar, but he is later

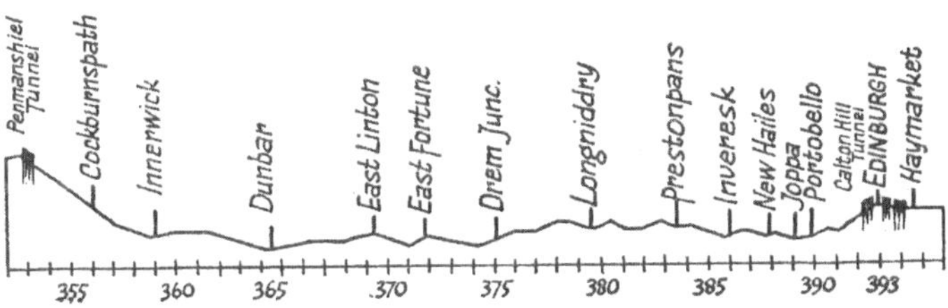

than he intended to be and drops the lever to 40 per cent.

This is the *Scotsman* ! There must be no mistakes ! 2750 responds with a louder roar from the chimney and Clarke with his shovel. A few shovelsful along the sides of the grate this time and a few more under the firehole to ' shake forward.' The needle moves over to 54 mph and stays there until Oakleigh Park is reached, a little less than half-way up, where it sticks for a moment, then falls to 51 at New Barnet and to 49 at Hadley Wood. Eldridge is watching it, but makes no move to check the fall, playing his old game of lost time against good fire, ' the trees and the wood ' that had puzzled MacKay. And consequently at the summit, Potter's Bar, the speed is down to 45.

Over the brow, however, the needle ceases to drop. It climbs steadily, reaching 75 as the train passes through Hatfield Station. 10.30½ a.m. – six minutes late ! Quite enough, but nothing to worry about, and as though to confirm his judgement, the safety-valves begin to stutter under the effects of Clarke's earlier firing and the easing of the load. Clarke takes advantage of this to get more water into the boiler, for the level has dropped to within an inch of the bottom of the gauge-glass during the climb up to Potter's Bar. Eldridge, for his part, eases the regulator. Langley water troughs are getting near. No sense in running over them at too high a speed – may tear the water scoop out of the bottom of the tender.

Shortly after passing over the classic arches of Welwyn Viaduct which spans the beautiful valley of the Mimram a hundred feet below, the speed is down to 60 mph. This is about right, and Clarke takes his stand at the scoop-operating wheel ready to lower it on the signal from Eldridge, whose head is just outside the window, watching for the zig-zag rail-side sign that marks the beginning of the trough.

Presently he holds his right arm out straight from the shoulder, and Clarke's attention is fixed upon this. The arm drops decisively. The scoop wheel spins round. And the train seems to surge forward onto the engine as, in fact, the engine is violently checked in speed under the impact of the scoop as this strikes the water.

The attention of both men now turns to the tender water gauge, a vertical pipe perforated at intervals throughout its length. Water begins to run from the lower holes and, as the level in the tender rises, from one after another of those higher up the pipe until within a few of the top, Eldridge calls ' Right ! '

The wheel is pulled round against the resistance of the water until the scoop is clear ; then locked to make sure that it will not work down of its own accord, and Clarke picks up his shovel once more.

For Eldridge, a glance across his gauges. Boiler pressure 210 lb. Good ! Pyrometer reading, 548º. Satisfactory ! Water-level, two-thirds of a glass. 2750 is in good fettle ! Clear now of the intricate signalling of the metropolis, he gives her her head.

The regulator is brought full open and the lever notched up to 30 per cent cut-off. The needle of the speed indicator begins to mount the scale. At the thirtieth mile post, just beyond Stevenage, it has recovered the 72 mph line ; at Hitchin, ancient town of lavender and roses, it passes the 78 mph line.

He notches up still further to 20 per cent, and the speed continues to rise as the train slips down the bank, shrieking with wide open whistle through Three Counties Station at 82½ mph. At Arlesey, the foot of the bank, the needle touches 90. She's running fast !

Both the position and attitude of Eldridge are slightly different now. It is impossible for him to keep his head out of the side window, and if it were possible he could not open his eyes to see in an air stream of such velocity. He gets up from his seat and stands as close as he can to the weatherboard spectacle (the front window), his hand resting lightly on the regulator handle. This would be snapped shut in a split second if the necessity arose. Tense with vigilance, he bends slightly forward to catch each signal as it passes, for at such a speed they flash by in a way that is frightening when the call may come to stop between one and the next.

' Passed the signal at danger ' is the blackest mark possible on any engine driver's record. There have been none on Eldridge's in nearly thirty years of driving. He intends there shall not be in the few more years that remain.

' Distant,' ' Home,' ' Starter ,' ' Distant,' ' Home,' ' Starter,' they seem to spring up from the ground. But he knows the exact position in which to look for each. Clarke, too, is tense to a degree in keeping with his lesser responsibility. The firing is heavy, but not all his time is being so spent and the rest of it finds him at his own spectacle, calling with monotonous regularity the aspect of each signal as it comes into view. ' Right,' ' Off,' ' Right,' ' Distant Off,' acknowledged each time by Eldridge with a nod.

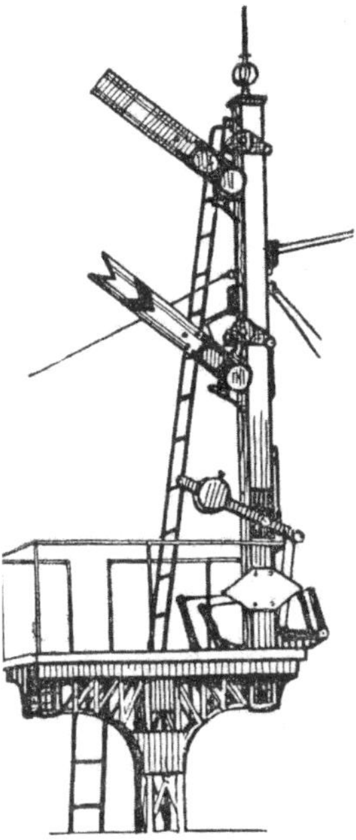

Signals for 2750 (introduced about 1931)

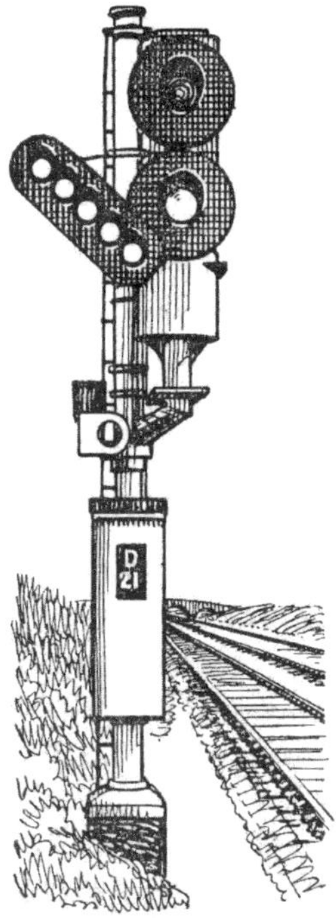

Colour light signals introduced about 1934 (modernised type, as this set, 1937)

Small wonder that the passenger in a British railway train is the safest passenger in the world.

The momentum of the train carries it over the hump beyond Arlesey with no loss of speed, then down again through the fertile loam of Bedfordshire's market gardens round Biggleswade and Sandy to reach 91 mph at the foot of St Neots rise. This mile-and-a-half of 1 in 330 up to the little market town on the border of Huntingdonshire checks the speed to 88, but it is back to 91 within two miles over the summit, and here Eldridge shuts the regulator.

Offord curve !

He looks over at the speed indicator as that formidable S bend is sighted. It stands at 85. Too fast ! The speed order for Offord is 70 mph, and it is an order that drivers with the experience of Eldridge respect. Offord ! A wicked left, right, left that will turn you over if it can.

His hand reaches to the brake application handle. There is the sharp hiss of in-rushing air ; then the drag of the train as the brake blocks apply.

75 mph, 73, 70, 68, the brake handle is lifted again to the 'release' position, the blocks drop away from the wheels, and the train rolls on and round the curve.

Clear of it, the exhaust roars again as the regulator is re-opened and at 11.1 precisely the *Flying Scotsman* runs through Huntingdon, two-and-a-half minutes late ; three-and-a-half minutes recovered between Hatfield and Huntingdon, the $26\frac{3}{4}$ miles from Hitchin covered in the even $18\frac{1}{2}$ minutes, giving an average speed of 86.5 mph.

Eldridge is well satisfied as he replaces his watch.

Stukely Bank follows, a three mile rise 1 in 200, that carries the line over the old Roman highway of Ermine Street, and this restricts the speed maximum to 71, but down through Abbots Ripton on the other side it is up again to 81, and fluctuates between that rate and 75. 2750 slips with graceful ease and purring exhaust through the Whittlesea Mere fen districts beyond Holme. In the distance appear those tall chimneys of the Fletton brickyards, largest in the world, soon left behind, and the train rumbles on to the fine lattice girder bridge across the River Nene to Crescent Junction, gateway to the cathedral city of Peterborough.

76¼ miles out from King's Cross ! Here there is a second and much more severe brake application to bring the speed down to the limit of 20 mph imposed by the track engineer.

Clear of the station and over the boundary into Lincolnshire, Eldridge does not yet attempt to recover any high speed on account of the approaching water troughs at Werrington, three-and-a-half miles beyond the station. Here the process of picking up water is repeated, and the needle then resumes its climb, reaching 71 mph at Essendine, the approach to Stoke Bank.

It is here that the load begins to be felt, for fourteen coaches is a heavy train. Clarke has well prepared : water at a high level in the glass ; a good fire-bed ; 210 lb. of steam pressure and 560° of superheat. The ascent begins with the regulator full open and cut-off at 35 per cent, steadily lengthened to 40 per cent, but the speed continues to fall past the 60 line as the train passes Little Bytham. Down still more to 43 per cent and then to 45 per cent, but even this cut-off does not check the loss of speed. Both steam pressure and water level are falling too, and at Corby the speed is down to 54 mph, but it is almost with unconcern that Eldridge drops the gear to 50 per cent. He knows he will not need to go lower than that. Though running late, he is not beyond his margin of recovery and will lose yet more time rather than ' punch ' his engine.

Stoke Box, the summit, is passed at 48 mph.

For every ' up ' there is a ' down,' and the ' down ' ahead is of some 27 miles, with stretches of 1 in 200, terminating with 11 miles of level running just beyond Newark. Rapidly the needle begins to climb again, and at Grantham it is back to 68 mph, a fine acceleration in five-and-a-half miles. Leaving the branches to Nottingham and Lincoln on left and right respectively, the *Flying Scotsman* is now racing northward well in the eighties, her fireman seated for a brief spell of rest after his exertions up Stoke Bank, her driver, close up to the weatherboard in his usual attitude, vigilant. Flashing through Peascliffe Tunnel and the little country stations of Hougham and Claypole she is across another boundary into Nottinghamshire and easing down to 80 for Newark-on-Trent. Through that, too, with a clattering of many wheels over the points of the one-time L.M.S. Nottingham-Lincoln branch, a quick dip in Muskham trough follows, close working this time between the two men, for Eldridge will not check below 70, and that is a high speed at which to take water from a trough.

No matter, though Clarke dare not try to fill the tanks he gets enough, and at the end of the level it is back to the nineties with 2750 making light work of it at 18 per cent cut-off and a full head of steam. Up now a little as the train enters the Dukeries country, and at the top of the hill a brief glimpse of Lincoln cathedral on the right. Over the level crossing with the old Great Central main line from Manchester to Grimsby, a crossing never made by Eldridge without recollection of the day when, as a young fireman, he was waiting to take up relief duties at Retford Station and saw the 1.10 p.m. out of London cut clean through a Grimsby-bound empty goods train, scattering wagons to left and right, and itself keeping the road and pulling up at the platform with no more damage than a broken carriage-window. On through the station and, still in the nineties, across the four-and-a-half mile Sutton plain to Ranskill, where a slight brake application is necessary to bring the speed down to 60 for Scrooby trough. A full tank must be got here after the short supply from Muskham. It is, and with brakes released, 2750 recovers to 70, up the three mile rise to Bawtrey, and to 85 down the other side. Then Eldridge shuts the regulator for Black Carr Junction, outpost of Doncaster, first town over the Yorkshire border, and beset by a formidable array of points and crossings for the Leeds and Bradford branches to the left, and those for Goole and Hull to the right.

A steady 65 through the station enables Eldridge to check his time by the platform clock. 12.34 p.m. – thirty seconds early ! Nice running !

He remarks : ‘ Reckon I dropped two climbing Stoke and made up three coming down. Might have been worse ! ’

The great works, birthplace of 2750, are left behind on the down side, and the train runs on. Level track for nearly eight miles beyond Arksey, and the speed steadily recovers from the Doncaster service check to 87 mph at Balne and fluctuates but little above or below that mark until the check again at Selby for the swing bridge. An opportunity follows to be getting a little margin in hand, and Eldridge will be running fast as he sights the signals for Chaloners Whin Junction,

At York Station

two miles short of York. Here he shuts the regulator and rolls on towards the great station through which, at this time, only the *Flying Scotsman* is booked to pass. Approaching the massive signal gantry that spans the whole of the line, there is a steady brake application and the train flows through the platform, quietly and with impressive grace, table lamps glowing through their red shades, passengers lunching and in easy conversation, most sparing a glance for the enormous clock on the footbridge, many commenting on the architecture of this fine station built on a sweeping curve, one of the most beautiful in the country and one destined on a not far distant day to be transformed into a mass of rubble, charred timbers and twisted steel girders, as hideous then as it is lovely now.

1.5 p.m. – three minutes early ! Doncaster to York, 32¾ miles in 31 minutes, an average of 62.4 mph. Comes York-to-Newcastle, the last lap of the journey. As well perhaps, for Clarke begins to tire. Over three hours of firing, during which he will have shifted little short of five tons of coal. But the going is easy now and, clear of the station, Eldridge opens up and 2750 responds as she did on the bank back at Potter's Bar.

Through Tollerton, half-way house for Edinburgh, and the place at which, when the ' Non-stop ' is running, the enginemen who have brought the train down from London pass back through the corridor tender to rest in the leading compartments, their places taken by the relief set. On to Alne, end of the eleven-mile stretch of level which sees the speed back to 75 mph, and Clarke's shovel again monotonously clanging against the firehole.

Thirsk, 22¼ miles, 23½ minutes, Northallerton passed

at 1.38 p.m., one-and-a-half minutes early. Wiske Moor trough and 3,000 gallons more water in the tender, and on through the Yorkshire dale country into County Durham at Croft Spa to reach Darlington at 1.50 p.m. with three minutes in hand. Careful running here across the Barnard Castle and Middlesbrough branches to left and right, then on again up short rises until just past

The swing bridge at Naburn

the crossing of the River Wear beyond Croxdale the majestic mass of Durham Cathedral rises into view and the station itself is passed, with speed still in the seventies at 2.14 p.m.

Downhill now all the rest of the way, but little chance of fast running, for the next ten miles is a maze of intersecting branches, colliery lines, and wagon ways serving the Durham coalfield.

No matter, there is plenty of time in hand, and pulling up the gear while leaving the regulator still full open,

Eldridge just keeps a taut drawbar and the train runs on towards the magnificent King Edward Bridge.

With the *click-click*, *click-click*, *click-click*, *click-click* of coach wheel over rail joint, made resonant by the vibrant bracing of the steel structure, 2750, sun aslant on gleam of brass and gloss of varnish, crosses the Tyne and brings the *Flying Scotsman* into Newcastle, drawing to a stand in Central Station quietly, unconcernedly, as though King's Cross was but a dozen miles back.

Eldridge draws out his cauliflower of a silver watch. 2.35 p.m. – one minute before time !

For a moment or two there is silence as he slowly wipes his hands on an engine-cloth, the silence of deep satisfaction in a job well done. Then he turns to his fireman.

' Nice run, mate ! '

But Clarke is a younger man, for whom life holds other interests than firing engines.

' Heavy going up Stoke ! Wonder what's on at the pictures.'

CHAPTER VI

HOT BOX!

IT was while working the up *Scotsman* from Newcastle to London towards the end of the summer that 2750 was first put out of service by that most dreaded of all locomotive ailments – the *hot-box*.

Peterborough had been passed with two minutes in hand and the train was running smoothly over the level stretch through Holme before it dawned on Fireman Clarke that he was using his slacker pipe to swill down the footboards quite an exceptional number of times and still was unable to put out the smouldering engine-cloth that seemed to have got down underneath them.

He tried again, driving the powerful jet of water well down between the outside board and the main frame with such vigorous perseverance that some of it splashed over the legs of Eldridge and brought his head in from the window.

Picturesquely describing his fireman's ineptitude he told him to get the pricker from the tender side and prise up the outside board so that he could play the jet underneath it.

Clarke obediently stepped to the cab side. This brought his head momentarily into the wind which carried to his nostrils the instant knowledge that the trouble was something far more serious than a smouldering engine-cloth.

He crossed quickly to Eldridge. ' Something's hot ! '

Eldridge eased the regulator but did not close it altogether. Always steady, he was careful to sight his next distant signal before getting up and going over to the window on the fireman's side. In a moment he was back again and had slammed shut the regulator, following up with a severe brake application which in a few seconds brought the speed of the train down to 45 mph.

Re-crossing to the right-hand side he put his head well outside in an endeavour to get a sight of the connecting rod.

' What is it ? ' asked Clarke.

' Can't see properly, but I don't think it's the rod ; afraid it's one of the boxes.'

' It is, replied Clarke, whose younger eyes had caught sight of it ; that tell-tale puff of thin blue smoke, blown out from between the spokes of the right-hand driving-wheel.

Eldridge saw the next one.

' Right driving box – and smoking hot. We're done for ! '

' Can't you get her through ? '

' Dare not try ! Tear the journal to bits ; might mean a new axle ! '

' What'll you do ? '

' Take on the pilot at Hitchin, confound the luck ! This is an engine failure, mate. Get me a small lump of coal.'

Tearing a sheet from his notebook and with one eye on the look-out for his signals he scribbled :

' 2750 *working up ' Scotsman ' failing with hot-box pilot required forward from Hitchin.*'

This he tied to the coal with a strand drawn from his engine-cloth, before wrapping both in it by tying the four corners together. As soon as the next signalbox came into sight he gave three short ' Crows ' on the whistle, the engine driver's signal of distress.

Almost immediately the signalman appeared on the balcony outside his box and as the train approached Eldridge made signs that he was going to throw out a message.

This brought the signalman to the bottom of the steps in time to see the cloth and its contents thrown from the footplate, landing thirty yards or so beyond the box.

Waving his hand as a sign that he had seen the drop he hurried forward, picked it up, untying it and reading the message on his way back.

Back in his box the movements of the signalman were quick and decisive. He went straight to the telephone : ' Control ? ... Hullo ... Control ? ... Farnbridge up box speaking ... Hullo ? ... Important message for Controller ... Right ? ... Engine 2750 working up *Scotsman* failed ... Yes ... No, running on but at reduced speed, passed here about thirty-five mph and two-and-a-half late ... Yes, hot-box ... Don't know, but pretty bad I think, saw smoke ... wants pilot forward from Hitchin, coming off. Don't know, but she'll be late ... fifteen minutes at her present speed, may be more ... Ought to make it without blocking the Leeds ... Just clearing my section, bell's ringing now ... All right ? ... Hanging up ! '

And so the wires begin to work and that complex but highly efficient organisation, a railway traffic control, to function.

They continue : ' Hullo ... Hullo ! ... Traffic Control

calling ... Hitchin Depot ? ... Superintendent, please ... Speaking ? ... Note up *Scotsman* failed Farnbridge, engine Number 2750 hot-box ... Trying to make your depot but ... will come off there ... pilot to work forward ... Are you ready ? ... Right.'

In his office at Hitchin the superintendent replaced his telephone receiver, but did not remove his hand from it ; almost at once he lifted it again, dialled, and : ' That Running Foreman Morrison ? Get ready for a quick change-over. 2750 has failed at Farnbridge with the up *Scotsman*, coming off here, our pilot forward. I'm going straight out to her now to see that she is all right. Meet me there.'

At the engine, standing on the stops in readiness for just such an emergency, depot superintendent and running foreman met.

' 2750 ? That will be Eldridge.'

' Yes, don't often have to come to *his* rescue.'

' No, Sir. What has he failed with ? '

' Hot-box.'

' That will take his engine away from him for a few days. We shan't find him in the best of tempers. He thinks a mortal lot of her.'

' Yes, I'm sorry. This one in good fettle ? '

' First class ! Washed out yesterday, oiled up and prepared and a clean fire.'

' Good, warn the enginemen. Fill her up and get full pressure ; they should be here inside the hour.'

' I'll see to it at once.'

' I want our men to make the change-over. Have them at the platform in readiness. Uncouple 2750 and bring her into the spur. Leave her there while they drop the pilot on to the train and couple up. I want Eldridge and his mate to have nothing to do but step off one engine onto the other. They will have come a long way and the last hour will have been rough for them. Coal all right ? '

' Good stuff, sir.'

' There's no more to be done now ; keep about the pilot and let me know as soon as the North Box gets the " Train entering Section " signal.'

' Very good ; I'll see to it. Fine chap, Eldridge ! '

And so were preparations made to meet the misfortune of 2750 still some 25 miles away.

Labouring a little, for the box has got very hot and is binding in the horn cheeks, the engine struggles on ; there is a heavy thump, thump, felt on the footplate, not unlike that felt in a motorcar when running on a flat tyre.

' Can't we get more oil to it ? '

' Wouldn't do much good,' replied Eldridge, ' at such a heat. It would burn at once and perhaps flash into fire ; but I'd give five quid for an ounce of graphite.'

Clarke took off his cap and flung it down.

' I'm going to try anyhow,' he said.

Eldridge looked at the speed indicator : 40 mph.

' All right, but keep your head well in and make dead sure of each foothold. I'll touch the whistle if anything comes along on the down road. Remember to screw the plunger up and not down.'

' Okay ! ' answered Clarke.

He swung himself round the handrail pillar of the cab side and, body braced against the wind pressure, moved steadily and carefully along the outside footplate, both hands grasping the handrail.

To Eldridge, tensely watching, it seemed a very long time before at last he reached the mechanical lubricator and stooping down lifted the top cover and removed the filter screen. To re-set the particular plunger to full feed was both a more difficult and a more dangerous operation by reason of the up-and-down movement of all twelve of them – miniature guillotines to sever as many fingers as might get in their path.

That Clarke had succeeded in doing so, however, was soon evident from the increased volume of the smoke coming from the axle-box and by that peculiarly pungent smell of burnt oil that always spells trouble to an engineman. Replacing the screen and cover he made his way cautiously back to the footplate.

‘ Thanks, mate,’ said Eldridge quietly.

Clarke nodded. Like Eldridge he knew that what he had done would have very little effect. He had done it as much for the man as for the machine and the man, to whom the machine was as a living thing akin to him, was grateful.

At Tempsford, the dull grinding of the journal in the box could be heard on the footplate and Eldridge pulled out his watch. 18 minutes late ! 20 lost in the 29 miles from Peterborough ! He hesitated, but only for a moment and then closed the regulator still more, reducing speed to 35 mph. He must get through to Hitchin somehow without damaging that journal beyond repair. The scored cuts it was sustaining could be machined out, but only if the deepest of them still left the diameter over minimum scrapping size.

The minutes were falling away now. At Biggleswade twenty-one had been dropped and at Arlesey, foot of the climb up to Stevenage, twenty-four. Sitting grim-faced in his seat Eldridge mentally ticked them off.

Five miles more – but uphill all the way and the speed fell to 32 mph, then 30 mph as 2750, crippled like a lame horse, ran on. What should have been the *roar* of her exhaust diminished to a bleat.

So different her progress now, driver and fireman both all but idle, no tense watching of signals, no anxious glancing at gauges or water levels, no vicious lurching as she strikes a crossing and no knife-like wind to cut their faces if put an inch over the cab side.

Instead, this heart-breaking, ignominious crawl that causes carriage-windows to drop and heads to emerge in questioning impatience – ' What's the matter with this train ? '

At Cambridge Junction within whistle range of the depot, Eldridge repeats his three-crow S O S. Pilot's pretty sure to be ready, but as well to be prepared. At Hitchin he brings the train to a stand in the platform at 5.10½ p.m., twenty-nine minutes late.

Awaiting him are the depot superintendent with the relief driver and fireman ; the latter jumping immediately down between tender and first coach to uncouple engine from train, the former climbing up into the cab to take over.

Coats slung over arms and food baskets in hand, Eldridge and Clarke descend to the platform.

'I'm sorry about this, Eldridge,' said the superintendent. ' We all know what 2750 means to you.'

' Thank you, sir. I'm sorry too. Means I'll lose her for maybe a week.'

' Oh, I don't know. Depends on the journal. You'll

have cut it a bit. The box is flaming hot. How far have you come with it like that ? '

' First noticed it at Holme, but it didn't get really hot until we reached Tempsford. Clarke here went round and opened the plunger to full feed.'

The superintendent nodded. While they had been

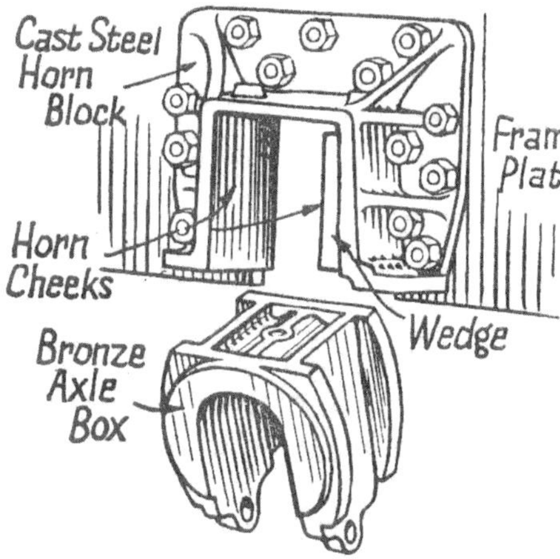

The axle box and where it goes

speaking 2750 was drawn off and the pilot engine, one of the older A1 class, No. 4478, was dropping back.

' We're putting on '78. She's a good engine, one of the best we have here, and you've my permission to take the last ounce out of her. You'll get back some of the time.'

Eldridge smiled, he knew what was meant.

' Thank you. I'll recover five minutes perhaps, but I don't think I could punch any engine beyond a little. You'll get mine up as soon as you can, won't you ? '

'Tonight, Eldridge, I promise you that. We'll examine her as soon as you've gone and cool the box. Ease off some of the weight and pack the keep with fresh oiled-waste. You can arrange up there for the wheel drop to be kept clear ; she'll be on it ready for the eight o' clock staff.'

With a metallic bump, 4478 was set back onto the train and the buck-eye coupled. The relief enginemen left the cab.

' Quick work, sir,' remarked Eldridge, looking at his watch as he stepped towards the cab. 5.14 ! The change-over effected in three-and-a-half minutes ; 32½ minutes late.

It seemed as if both men were lifted out of their inertia ; Clarke, in an unleashed burst of suppressed energy had the fire to his liking in the first four minutes, and from the standing start half-way up the 1 in 200 climb, Arlesey to Stevenage, the train was running at 52 mph at the summit. Thence the track is undulating as far as Welwyn, and the speed rose to 71 mph at Woolmer Green, passed the 82 line at the Garden City, and reached 91 as the fourteen coaches swung round the curve into Hatfield Station. Utilising to the utmost the momentum that he now had behind him, Eldridge dropped the lever of the engine to a 50 per cent cut-off, notwithstanding the speed at which the train was running, for the five mile rise to Potter's Bar and passed it still in the nineties, though with the boiler pressure ' knocked back ' to 160 lb. per square inch, for even the furious firing of Clarke could not avail to hold the needle against so tremendous a demand for steam.

No matter, downhill now right into King's Cross, and as the lever was brought up again the pressure began to

Hadley Wood at 90 mph

recover, enabling 4478 to hold her speed and put the train through Wood Green Tunnel at the even 90 mph.

Here, Eldridge reluctantly eased the regulator. Too close in for such fast running. Short sections ; suburban trains on adjacent lines. 80 at Hornsey ; 70 at Harringay ; 60 at Finsbury Park, and then – King's Cross 5.39 p.m. Twenty-four minutes late.

No less than eight-and-a-half minutes of the lost time had been regained over the 32 miles Hitchin to King's Cross, which had been covered at an average speed of 76.8 mph.

For a long time afterwards the two men used to refer to that finish as ' The flight from Hitchin.'

True to his promise the superintendent at Hitchin, after first-aid attention to the axle-box, had 2750 worked up light during the night at a speed not exceeding 20 mph, and in the early hours of the morning she limped home. Here the fire was thrown out of the fire-box and the smoke-box cleared.

The little shed shunting engine then coupled up and like a tug manoeuvring an ocean liner, pushed and pulled with much puffing and hissing, until the disabled giant was set with the driving wheels fairly in the middle of the electric wheel-drop table in the repair shop. The shunting engine uncoupled again and proceeded to its lesser duties.

The foreman fitter was a little surprised when he took duty that morning to see the wheel-drop occupied, and by what, but after a preliminary look round, he lost no time in rearranging his programme of work so that the invalid received priority over all other repairs, and in less than fifteen minutes the wheel-drop gang were at work.

First, off with the side rods, both sides ! They were drawn carefully forward from the crank pins and lowered to the floor. Next a couple of fifteen-ton hydraulic jacks under the leading buffer beam ; up with it about three inches ; packing pieces on top of the leading coupled axle-boxes then drop it again. Main frames carried on the axle-box crowns now, and the spring gear does not have to support the additional load as the driving wheels are lowered slowly until the boxes rest on the horn stays. Connecting rods are dismantled and the attached piston of each pushed up to the front end of the cylinder as far as it will go, taking the big ends forward too, out of the way. Now the wheels are turned a little to bring the middle journal so that it will clear the end of the connecting rod as the table goes down. Up first though, an inch or two above rail level to ease the load off the spring gear, then with the hangars and the centre pin of the buckle taken out, the springs are lifted down on to a board laid across the rails to bridge the pit and from there barrowed away. Only the horn stays to strip now whilst the weight is off them, then we're ready to lower out.

The four vertical screwed pillars that carry the girdered table spin round with the clangour of meshed pinions, lowering the table with the driving wheels on it at the rate of four-and-a- half feet per minute. Roughly half-way down, the girders strike the ends of bar links connected through chains to wheeled runners which ride upon short girder-section runways and carry the rails, which by this means are brought towards each other as the table descends until, when it has reached its lowest limit, they form, with the pit rails, one continuous length over which by means of a rope and capstan 2750 is drawn off clear of the wheel-drop.

Again the screwed pillars spin round, but this time in the reverse direction, and the table rises up in the pit, the rails above separating under the pull of balance weights, out of its way. At the top, the pair of wheels are rolled off and forward to the axle-box bench.

Here both boxes are swung round on the axle until the keep is uppermost ; a few smart blows drive out the keep pins and the boxes fall to the ground with the axle journals exposed.

This is the moment for which the foreman has been waiting, callipers in hand, much as a doctor with his stethoscope. Carefully he taps and tries, taps and tries until he has the ' feel ' to a sixty-fourth of an inch of the diameter at the deepest of several nasty scores that ring the journal. Anxiously he reads off the span of the callipers on a steel rule – $8\frac{11}{16}$ inches, three-sixteenths of an inch over scrapping size ! A near thing but – all right !

He lifts his arm, and overhead a big thirty-five ton girder crane rumbles into movement and travels towards him, the carriage traversing the girders at the same time so that when it stops, the massive bull's horn hook is directly over the wheels. Down it comes, the two chains are looped each round the rim of a wheel, then up again and away rumbles the crane to the other end of the shop, the wheels dangling and swinging in mid-air with the pathetically helpless appearance of a kitten being carried by a cat.

Arrived over the wheel-lathe the hook lowers slowly and carefully this time, until the axle is ' centred ' in the machine ; then, with chains unlooped it is up and away again until the next call.

The operating table has been reached !

The lathe motor whines on a rising note as the current is switched on, the wheels begin to revolve and as the keen-edged cutting tool traverses to and fro along the length of the defaced journal, the deep and ugly grooves that have been cut into it are gradually planed out until it is bright as polished glass once more, true and parallel to one-thousandth of an inch, all trace of the damage gone.

Meantime an inquest is proceeding with the superintendent himself as coroner. What made that axle-box get hot ? It is necessary that the cause should be definitely established for there are not so many engines allocated to his district that he can afford to have them lying on operating-tables instead of hauling trains. Moreover a delay from such a cause constitutes an engine failure, and must be reported to headquarters to the possible detriment of his standing at the head of the divisional list for reliability.

With his foreman he tests the oil stream, knowing from long experience that this is the most likely place to find a clue. The pipe feeding the right-hand driving axle-box is disconnected close up under the mechanical lubricator and a specially made force pump applied to the freed end. His finger over the other feels the pressure build up, and when he releases it the flush of oil compressed in the pipe gives him clear evidence that there is neither blockage nor leakage. A sound line, but he remembers the case of 5814 a year or two back when, after endless searching, the blockage was ultimately traced to the feed hole of the lubricator sleeve itself. Best make sure. Even Eldridge, if he is in a hurry, is not above taking out the screw and charging the reservoir direct from his eight-pint oil-bottle, dirt and all.

The pipe is reconnected and the wheel of the lubricator spun round by hand while both men watch the open end where, sure enough, after a while a few drops of oil appear, later to run in a steady unbroken stream.

Reluctantly, for they know it may be difficult now to get on to the track of the cause, they leave the engine.

'Let's have a look at the box.'

This is wiped down for their inspection and they look closely at the side faces that slide up and down in the horn blocks. Though badly burned and discoloured it is clear that there has been no kind of seizing even in slight degree, and the box is swung over bore uppermost.

No white metal or trace of white metal, so completely has it melted and vanished, the bare serrations that anchor it appear clean as when they were cut.

Are they deep enough ? Often shallow metal has proved to be the cause of heating. Axle-boxes are metalled and bored, metalled and bored and each time a cut comes off the gun metal casting, and the depth of the metal grows less. Then a thickness is reached which is insufficient to withstand the load upon it : a crack appears followed by another, then another until a piece is separated. After that, disintegration of the entire bearing is certain and rapid, and overheating inevitable.

They measure the depth carefully, one-eighth of an inch : thin certainly, but not too thin. The search must be continued, a difficult case. Only the keep remains.

This does not seem likely to reveal very much, half-filled with mis-shapen lumps of solidified white metal, chips of gun-metal and the charred remains of the Armstrong oil pad, the frame of which lies twisted and bare. The foreman stoops to pick it up for closer examination, but is stopped.

‘ Don’t touch it for a moment. Which part of the journal was most deeply scored ? ’

‘ The wheel boss end. There was a groove cut about two inches from the face of the boss that was almost three-sixteenths of an inch deep.’

‘ Then I think we’ve got it.’

His chief bent down and pointed to the brightened head of a rivet that had secured the fabric of the pad to the outer concave steel strip.

‘ That’s been bearing directly on the journal,’ He lifted the frame from the keep and it could be seen that the rivet head had been practically worn away.

‘ But the pad would be between them ; that is, until it was burnt away and that must have been after the heating had occurred.’

‘ Ought to have been, but it’s clear that it wasn’t. You’ll find that at the last periodical examination of the axle-boxes, this one for some reason was missed and the old pad was left in. Already too long in service it wore through to the rivet and the damage was done. Find out from the examination records who was the fitter responsible and send him in to see me.’

At the other end of the repair shop a cracked, discoloured and metalless axle-box lies on the scrap heap, but in a nearby lathe chips of gold and silver fall from the new one that is being bored out, later to be bedded down to the newly-turned journal.

Then the wheels roll back again on to the wheel-drop table and are lowered into the pit ; the engine is brought into position over them and carefully they are raised, the axle-boxes eased into the horn cheeks, spring gear rec-connected, and the job is done. Not quite ! A test of the weight distribution is necessary following its derangement by uncoupling the springs and the engine is hauled across the yard to the weigh-bridge for the weight on each pair of wheels to be checked over and adjusted where this proves to be necessary.

The whole repair has not taken very long, and when the patient is back once more in her shed stall, it is more by design than accident that the shop foreman encounters Driver Eldridge as the latter is coming on duty that afternoon.

'Bad luck about that journal on 2750,' he says.

'What way, mate ?'

'You cut it too deep, I've had to send the wheels to main shops. Means a new axle, I'm afraid.'

Eldridge was justifiably downcast on receiving this information.

'Will it be a long job, do you think ?'

'Anything from a month to six weeks. They're pretty busy in the Works on new construction ; we'll have to wait our turn. I doubt if you'll get her again for some time,' he says, and passes on.

There is a wisp of steam from the safety-valves as Eldridge clears the corner of the office building. 2750 will not be late off shed this day.

Chapter VII

A HEAVY LOAD

The working lives of enginemen are not in every hour of every day battles against ill-luck. Hot bearings, bad coal, furred tube-plates, fog, dragging brakes, burst tubes, blown joints – these are ills encountered by them all at some time or other. But far more often is a day's work entirely uneventful. A start ' On time ' with a moderate load usually ends, given skill and vigilance on the journey, in an arrival ' On time ' and although always full of interest and, for the firemen, arduous, the days of these men leave them for the most part quiet and very contented.

Some such thoughts were in the mind of top-link driver Robert Eldridge as on one spring afternoon, with arms resting on the beading of his rear cab-window, he looked back along the length of No.10 platform lazily watching the bustle and stir of entraining passengers and platform staff, his mate standing by the cab door doing the same. It was the fifteen-minute pause that always occurs between coupling on to a train and the guard's ' Right away.' Everything ready ; fire level and well past the ' green ' ; water showing two-thirds in the gauge-glass ; pressure just beginning to set up a throb in the Ross ' pop ' safety valves ; and vacuum train-pipe gauge dead steady on the 21 inch mark.

The train, the 4.45 p.m. King's Cross to Newcastle, worked through by 2750, had loaded only thirteen coaches, made up principally of those fine Gresley thirty-nine-ton composite coaches and a triple-articulated dining-car set, the total running to 520 tons, just comfortable pulling that accounted largely for the placid outlook of Eldridge and the altogether out-of-character good temper of his usually explosive companion.

The latter flicked open his live-steam injector to check the impending lift of the safety valves and the nervy shattering roar of escaping steam that would follow, and turned back to Eldridge.

'Mixed lot tonight, Bob; by the look of some of 'em the cars will be well-patronised.'

'Well, why shouldn't they be?'

'No reason, only I'd sooner be there with 'em than here with you. They can thank their stars I'm not on your side of the footplate.'

'And why?'

'Because if I was, I'd see I hit Offord curve at ninety and landed the soup in their laps.'

'You're a friendly soul, Jack. Wonder what's on the mind of Tom Beckley? He's looking more self-important than ever.'

Tom Beckley, one of the station inspectors, was walking briskly and in a very business-like manner down the platform.

'Coming to tell us he's been appointed General Manager, I expect.'

'Don't know about that, but it looks like he's coming here.'

'Why should he?'

'Don't know, unless he's bringing a Form One to you for pinching that new coal pick.'

'I didn't pinch it, it's the old one re-shafted. Do

you get Form Ones for having new handles put in your picks ? '

Beckley approached the footplate.

' 'Afternoon, Driver Eldridge, you're wanted on the phone in our office at once.'

Eldridge turned to his mate with a look of incredulous surprise.

' 'S'pect it's the missus presented you with a fine bouncing baby.'

Beckley repeated ; ' Come on ! He said " At *once* ".'

' Who did ? '

' Your boss, the District Loco Superintendent.'

For an instant Eldridge still hesitated, then from force of habit glanced at his brake gauge, cylinder cock operating lever and reversing gear.

' Pull her up to mid-gear,' he said to Clarke, ' and watch everything. You're responsible for this engine until I come back, and she's coupled to a train with 400 passengers aboard.'

With which he stepped down from the footplate and walked quickly back with the inspector to his office where on the desk lay the cup-like receiver of a wall telephone.

Somewhat gingerly Eldridge picked it up and after a distasteful glance at this unfamiliar contraption, put it up to his ear, and advancing to the mouthpiece of the instrument on the wall said, for want of anything better to say : ' Yes ? '

His superintendent's voice came through the receiver, words slowly spoken and carefully articulated.

' That you, Eldridge ? '

' Yes, sir.'

' I want you to listen carefully. What I have to say is very important and there isn't much time.'

' Yes, sir.'

' 2744, engine for the 5 p.m. Leeds has turned over at the Outlet, fouling both roads. All movements into and out of the loco. yard are completely blocked and will be until we can lift her clear, which won't be done inside two hours.'

' Sounds bad, sir.'

' It is bad, the immediate worst being that the engine which should be down there at the station setting back on to its train, is up here at the loco. lying on its side, and no other can get by to take its place. The station pilot worked the four-ten.'

' Have to cancel the train, won't they ? '

' So I'm advised on all sides, but I've never had to cancel a main line express train yet for want of an engine and I'm not going to begin now.'

' But what else can you do, sir ? '

' I can put your Newcastle back fifteen minutes and send both trains away as one at five o'clock behind you.'

' You mean . . . but I could never get them there ; I could never lift them ; I'd not get to Finsbury Park with a load like that.'

' This isn't a panic decision of mine, Eldridge, I have weighed the situation up carefully, and I think you could. No other engine and perhaps not many other enginemen, but 2750 is the finest locomotive ever built at Doncaster Works, and you and Clarke between you can get out of her every ounce she's got. Had there been any other engine at all on the four forty-five today, or for that matter, any other enginemen, the five o'clock would be cancelled, but with the combination I have got I am going to take a chance and I ask for your help.'

' I'll do what I can, of course, sir.'

' Thanks Eldridge, now listen. These are the arrangements. You stand in Number 10 with thirteen on, five-hundred-and-twenty tons ; the five o' clock is in Number 12 with eleven on ; four-hundred-and-forty tons ; your combined train will weigh roughly nine-hundred-and-sixty tons, nothing like which load has ever before been worked out of King's Cross behind a single locomotive, but no matter.

' Fortunately, the five o'clock cars were worked in by a J52 six-coupled shunting tank, just the type we needed to help you out of the station. It has been fixed up with the Traffic people for him to propel you out, through Gas Works Tunnel and up as far as Belle Isle box. If you need him farther, give three crows and he will keep with you through Copenhagen Tunnel in case you slip. The rails are always greasy there.

' Then he must drop off, and it will be up to you on to Grantham. You will come off on arrival, if you ever reach it, and the train will be divided again into its Newcastle and Leeds sections with two Grantham Pacifics working forward. You will be advised as to your return working.

I want you to understand, Eldridge, that the responsibility for this gamble – and it is a gamble – is wholly mine. Whatever delay or mishap may result I shall answer for, and not you. What I want you to do is to combine all your skill and experience as a driver, with the power of a very fine engine, and see if you can pull this load of nearly a thousand tons from King's Cross to Grantham.'

' I shall have a very good try, sir, and if it can be done I shall do it, but what about Stoke Bank ? '

' Stoke Bank is the throw upon which the whole stake depends. That you will get as far as that, though late, I am in no doubt whatever, but whether or not you will be able to climb it I have, quite honestly, no idea at all. You may or you may not. None of us knows what 2750 is really capable of. Break her if you must, only get her up. Understand ? '

' Yes, sir.'

' Right. That's all Eldridge, and good luck.'

With another glance at the ear-piece as if it were a particularly vicious kind of insect, Eldridge laid it down again on the desk, to be reached for and hung up by Inspector Beckley.

He walked out of the office and back along the platform to his engine without a word.

There he gave his fireman the gist of the conversation that had taken place, quite expecting that that hasty-tempered young man would blue the air with the vehemence of his opinion of the proposal and flatly refuse to put it into effect, but in this he was wrong.

Clarke was at first incredulous, then pitying, as behoves a sensible man who suddenly finds himself surrounded by lunatics, but after that he was – interested.

900 odd tons ! Well, why not have a shot at it ? Here would be a battle calling for all his young strength, all his skill, and all his endurance. As the idea became more fixed his interest grew until it was almost with enthusiasm that he turned seriously to Eldridge.

' All right, mate, I'm game to put up a good fight for it.'

Eldridge was considerably surprised by this reception

of his tidings, but was too concerned with the task that lay before him to do more than nod his head, and both men were silent as they waited the passing of the few remaining minutes to 4.45.

It came, and with it the guard's signal, 2750 pulling out of No.10 past the coaches of the 5 o'clock standing engineless and forlorn in Number 12, and on through the cross-over just in front of the tunnel. Clearing it, the train stopped and not without causing raised eyebrows and anxious glances from unenlightened passengers set slowly back into 12, the dull thud and bunching coaches indicating a clean lock of the buck-eye coupling. 2750 stood in the tunnel – and in it by two coach lengths.

Once before, during some tractive-effort trials of a new Gresley design, the 2-8-2 *Cock o' the North*, an engine had stood out to within a few yards of the tunnel mouth, but never before had the length of a train put an engine inside it.

The demeanour of both men on the footplate was now utterly different from that good-natured bonhomie that usually obtained between them ; both were very serious and very intent.

Clarke broke a long silence.

'I'm not so bad with a shovel, but you've been longer at the game than I have ; are there any tips you can pass on ? For this trip, anyway, I'll pay attention to anything that anybody can tell me.'

Eldridge was careful not to reveal the surprise he felt at this uncommon assumption of humility on the part of his mate ; he answered soberly :

'If I were you I'd run a black fire ; keep it as thick as you can and only let it burn through when we're running down hill. You'll need the weight of a black fire, if you let it get thin the terrific blast will pick it up off the bars and fling it out of the chimney.'

' For the same reason keep the firehole door open about six inches all the time. That way you'll get some of the air drawn in through the door instead of through the fire.'

' But what about the tubes ? You've always said that drawing in cold air through the door straight on to the tubeplate sets up contraction and makes the tubes leak.'

' So it does Jack, and so it will this time, but the Guv'nor's words to me were " Break her if you must." I shan't do that, but I'll spring the tubes to save your fire, it's the only way you'll keep it on the grate.'

' Anything else ? '

' No, work your injectors by the road, but you don't need me to tell you that. Help me by easing them off when she's all out, and I'll help you by notching her up when your glass is dangerously low.'

A face appeared at the cab window.

' I'm the driver of 3872 at the bottom of Twelve. I've orders to propel you as far as Belle Isle Box, and by the look of things you're going to want it.'

Eldridge was not responsive.

' I may need you through Copenhagen ; if I do I'll give you three crows as we pass the Isle.'

' All right, in that case I'll drop off as we clear it ; how are you off for sand ? '

' Plenty when we left the shed. Now will you recouple your vacuum and blow up from your end while I do it from mine. I want the whole brake system cleared of air, and it's a long train.'

' I'll say it is,' and the face withdrew.

' Know who filled those sand-boxes, Jack ? '

' I did.'

' Good ; to the lids ? '

' All but ; I'm satisfied we've got enough, but I think I'll jump down and try 'em.'

Clarke climbed down into the six-foot, hammer in hand. As Eldridge opened the steam and dry-sand gear-valves, Clarke tapped the sand pipes sharply to dislodge any damp or congealed sand. Satisfied, he returned to the footplate.

' How are we going to get the " Right away " in here ? '

' A relief guard will come up to us. Can you see the starting signal for Number 12 ? '

' Yes, and it's " off ".'

Eldridge took a last look round the cab, noted the pressure-gauge needle hovering over the 220 lb. mark ; dropped his gear down to ' full fore,' and waited.

Not for very long ; a thin piping whistle sounded in the darkness of the tunnel and looking back he saw a guard approaching, vigorously waving his green flag.

' Right ! ' said Clarke, arm outstretched.

A short blast on the whistle, answered from the other end ; a soft tug on the regulator and the train began to move.

It was moved a good deal more by the noisily-important little engine in the rear than by the relatively quiet big one in the front, for the 4 feet 8 inch coupled wheels of the shunter were better suited to start such a load than the 6 feet 8 inch ones of the Pacific, also for all that the sand boxes were full, every ounce of it would be needed later, and Eldridge did not intend to use it before he must. So 3872 puffed and pushed as he brought up the gear to 45 per cent cut-off and continued to puff and push when at Belle Isle Box the driver received and acknowledged the agreed three-crow whistle.

The train was well out through Copenhagen when the men felt the rearward surge as the full load sat back on the drawbar of 2750 ; it was countered by Eldridge jerking out the regulator handle with a snap to the full open quadrant stop and running down the gear to 50 per cent. This checked the rapid retardation, and content with it for the present he held on. It also set back the needle from 220 lb. to 200 lb. per square inch and started Clarke on a left, right, left, right swing that was to continue virtually without pause for the next two-and-a-half hours.

At Finsbury Park the indicator was recording 40 mph, lifted only a further 5 at Wood Green, foot of the Potter's Bar rise, and then it began steadily to fall, for it was far too early in the game for any overloading that might affect the fire, or for that matter the engine, later on. Already there was an ominous roar at the chimney and, still at 50 per cent cut-off, 2750 was feeling the strain. At Oakleigh Park, half way up, the speed had dropped to 35 and at Hadley Wood to 30. Entering the north tunnel Eldridge opened the sand valve for the first time. A bad tunnel this, with a perpetual leak through the roof from a concealed spring that kept the rail surfaces always treacherously greasy !

As they emerged, the speed was down to 25, but Eldridge made no move to recover it. This was a train that would have to be ' played ' just as an angler plays a hooked salmon. He wouldn't waste the power of 2750 trying to accelerate a 960 ton load up a 1 in 200 bank. Let her go, as the salmon is let go, but always within limits. Twenty-five miles an hour was within that limit in these special circumstances, even for a main-line express train northbound for Newcastle. The road would favour them soon, and that would be the time to move a little faster.

Two coach lengths inside Potter's Bar Tunnel and with a shudder she slipped, checked in a flash by Eldridge who, keyed up as he was, had anticipated the possibility and was ready. Damp rails again. He left the sand running until out of the tunnel, and half-a-mile farther on had put the engine over the brow of the hill and begun the drop down to Hatfield.

He did not touch the gear. Clarke seemed able so far to hold the needle about the 200 line with a 50 per cent cut-off ; he would cash his mate's skill and muscle into momentum. If once he could get that enormous weight moving at 60 or 70 miles an hour its sheer impetus would carry it well up the hills.

And the engine was responding to the change of grade. Slowly, very slowly, the indicator needle was moving over the scale, and at Hatfield had reached the 51 mph. mark, rising to 55 as the bottom of the bank was passed. The ensuing rise to Woolmer Green brought it back to 46, but then there was the four-and-a-half mile stretch of undulating track profile to Stevenage, passed at 51 again.

Here, Eldridge pulled up the gear first to 40 per cent and then to 30 per cent. It was a drastic shortening but he did it to ease the frightening effort of his mate Jack Clarke, who without word or look seemed to swing left and right like a machine but, Eldridge knew, he was not a machine and could not, without collapse, maintain such an output.

The next 30 miles or so to Huntingdon were down grade, good stretches of 1 in 200, 300, and 400 ; in them Eldridge hoped to get a final speed of between 70 and 80 mph ; enough momentum to carry him up and over Stukeley Bank and well on towards Peterborough.

He notched up to thirty and within two minutes a sharp Bang ! told Clarke that the safety-valves had lifted for the first time since leaving King's Cross. Looking up he convinced himself of the good news ; checked the gauge-glass reading at half full, and all but fell into the bucket seat provided for him : too exhausted to bother about slacking down the coal dust, of which there was plenty, or even to pull forward some coal on the tender which was getting too far back now for him to reach comfortably, in spite of the self-trimming coal space.

Eldridge dropped the lever down a little to check the escaping steam and steadily set himself to build up speed ; to pull in his line. The first five miles beyond Stevenage are graded at 1 in 200 down, and at Arlesey, the bottom, the needle of the speed indicator had climbed from the 51 to the 64 mark. Not spectacular acceleration, certainly, but he was well satisfied as he glanced across at Clarke, sitting relaxed.

The short hump beyond Arlesey had no effect on the speed, and with the lever a little more down now Biggleswade was passed at 68 and Tempsford at 71. A slight fall to 69 over the St Neots hump, then up again to 72 at Offord and a final spurt took the train through Huntingdon at a fraction over 74 mph.

So far so good, Eldridge now had in his heavy train an

accumulated momentum that would carry him through a lot of adverse grade, and he was 59 miles out from King's Cross, just a little more than half way on his journey.

But he was at the bottom of his hill and at the foot of Stukeley Bank, three miles of 1 in 200, up this time instead of down.

He decided to draw a little at any rate on this enormous reserve of kinetic energy and breasted the bank with the lever at 45 per cent only (the regulator handle, still full over, had not been touched since the train emerged from Copenhagen Tunnel), deciding it would be better to lose speed than to shake up the fire-bed, appreciably thinner now since Clarke's respite. The latter, with a good level of water now showing in the gauge-glass, had shut his live steam injector and was preparing to climb up into the tender coal-space with his coal pick to bring more of the bright lumps forward to mix with the small. Eldridge stopped him with the shouted word ' Stukeley,' the first to pass between them on that trip and pointing to the pressure-gauge took up the coal pick himself.

Clarke, seeming scarcely to understand, changed pick for shovel and resumed his deadly monotonous swinging and placing. Two for the left back corner, two for the right, three close up under the door. Three along the left side of the firebox, three along the right side, and now for the throwing. ' How my wretched arms ache ! ' Two well up in the left front corner, two well up in the right, two over the drop grate. ' Six feet long this grate.'

Next a shading of the glare from the firehole door with a clever twisting of the blade of his shovel as ' Fill up the holes, then start all over again.' Yes ! three bad places, bright patches with high leaping flames, thin places that are letting what is relatively cool air rush through into the tubes. Two for that one up in the middle front. ' It *would* be there ! ' Three for the two holes forming together in the centre of the fire-bed. A final look over the surface. ' Level enough and even enough.' A grateful straightening of his back and Clarke remembers the coal pick and his need to use it.

He looks round to find it gone, and his driver too ; both are atop of the tender. Eldridge, head turning back to sight his signals, has taken advantage of the short climb up Stukeley to bring forward some coal for his mate. With almost forgotten skill the pick end of the coal hammer is buried in the mass of coal. A sudden jerk brings forward a small slide of lumps and dust alike. A slick twist of the wrist as his arms reach the top of their lift and, with a crack, down comes the face end instead of the pick end, first on this piece then on that, which, struck parallel with the cleavage planes of the coal, split from seventy – or eighty pound lumps into nuggets of five or six.

Another backward glance for signals, another slide, then crack, crack.

Clarke stood a moment watching him with something very nearly akin to affection, then crossed over to the driver's side to sight the distant for Abbots Ripton that would shortly come into view round the bend. He saw it ' OFF ' ; lifted his hand to Eldridge ; opened the steam cock of his live ejector, then on again. Two for the left back corner, two for the right, three close up under the door. . . .

Over Stukeley and down the other side ; practically

level running now for the eighteen miles to Tallington, foot of Stoke, but with 960 tons on the drawbar, this meant very little to 2750, to Driver Eldridge or to Fireman Clarke, particularly as the service compulsory slackening to 20 mph through Peterborough meant virtually starting all over again.

Still, at Helpston Box, after picking up water from Werrington troughs, that incomparable trio had recaptured the even 60 mph and the great climb began.

As Eldridge knew it would, the momentum of such an enormous weight even at that relatively moderate speed carried him well up and it was not until the four-and-a-half mile stretch of 1 in 200 was encountered that the lever began to drop. A mile beyond Little Bytham it was down to 50 per cent cut-off, and the speed to 48 mph.

With a glance at the pressure-gauge he let it continue to fall, for precious as momentum was, boiler pressure was more so, and the needle was on the wrong side of the 180 lb. per square inch mark. Reaching forward he opened the valve of the sand gun and a stream of fine sand was sprayed over the firebox tubeplate and carried forward through the tubes clearing them, as could be seen by the black shower ejected from the chimney, of soot and fine ash clinkered in the form of ‘ crow’s-nests ’ on the tube ends. It helped a little and the needle moved over to the 200 mark, but speed was down now to 40, and at Corby, three miles from the summit, to 31.

Clarke’s swing now had taken on a faster rhythm, and the strain was telling as his white-streaked, grim and sweating face made all too plain. It caused Eldridge to hesitate before he lengthened the cut-off still more. But

' Break her if you must, only get her up,' the Guv'nor had said, and besides, what would happen if he couldn't ? A light engine, he supposed, would be sent up from Grantham with a ' Wrong Line Order ' to hook on the front and haul him into the station like a broken-down lorry.

The thought decided it and he ran down the wheel, not to 55 per cent or to 60 per cent, but to the limit, 65 per cent cut-off ; full regulator. Twenty-seven-Fifty, for the first time since she had been built, was ' all out ' ; she had ' got the lot ! '

But Eldridge had failed to understand fully what such a load as he was pulling really meant ; with the ' way ' of the train lost it was as if he were coupled to a liner. When he ran down the lever the response was immediate – but it was only in the deafening roar of the exhaust from the chimney ; the speed continued to fall.

In less than two minutes the needle passed over the 20 mph line, and as it reached 13, Clarke slammed shut the firehole door on a ' black ' fire. His rate of firing had been so high that it had resulted in the very rare occurrence of blacking out the entire surface of the fire-bed with raw coal. Except for an occasional small tongue of flame it was completely without incandescence and might from its appearance be a lifeless coal dump. The enormous draught that so late a cut-off would put through the fire would very soon have the fire-bed a white-hot furnace again, but by then they would either be stalled on the Bank or running into Grantham. Whichever way it went Clarke had shot his bolt now and was done. He flung his shovel up into the tender and crossed over to Eldridge.

' Will she do it ? '

Eldridge shrugged and spread his arms. He too could do no more. Every inch of the lever ! Every ounce of steam ! Both men were helpless.

The issue lay between Engine No. 2750 and 960 tons.

Just past the ninety-ninth mile post, one mile from the summit, the needle fell to 6 mph – through 5 and on to 4 mph !

Walking pace ! The 4.45 p.m. King's Cross to Newcastle !

Eldridge's eyes were on the needle (no need now to look out for signals) and he saw it as it wavered a little and then held.

With such factors as internal resistance, rail friction and wind resistance practically eliminated by the negligible speed the whole power output of the locomotive was available for lifting the train, and the equation balanced. Without any doubt now, if she did not slip, 2750 would reach the summit.

If she did not slip ! both enginemen realised that it all turned on that, but still there was nothing that they could do. By leaning well out from the cab door Clarke could see and report the precious unbroken golden yellow ribbon of crushed sand that covered the rail surface. Would it enable the 60 tons of weight in those six-coupled wheels to keep their grip ? It was hard to predict, for the turning moment on them was indeed tremendous, each blast of exhaust steam was exploded out of the chimney with the velocity and detonation of a field gun, and as each of the three cranks right-angled its connecting rod the engine surged forward so that its slow progression took the form of a series of short, sharp jerks.

They waited ; Eldridge hand on regulator to snap it shut at that first tremble which presages slip.

And they slowly climbed, until the rounding of a slight left-hand curve revealed the sharp, horizon-like outline that marked the summit, the track and banks on each side of it seeming to form a silhouette, gradually drawing nearer.

The struggle of 2750 to reach it was almost human to watch, the ‘ yaw ’ of her head from side to side as first left and then right cylinder forced it over was very like the shaking of a swimming dog's, hard pressed. What should have been live cinders ejected from the chimney were in fact small lumps of raw coal lifted bodily from the fire-bed and sucked through the tubes by the sheer ferocity of the blast which shook the fire-hole door-catch in its rack so that it set up a rattling din, out-shouted only by the thunder from in front.

But the enginemen could see over the brow now and Stoke Tunnel entrance rose into view. As they looked back along the train, its last coaches still not yet round the bend, it seemed incredible that the little white gradient post that marked the summit of Stoke Bank and the highest point on what was once the Great Northern Railway could be passing by the footplate.

Coach by coach as the train, too, passed it, Eldridge pulled up the gear. Not to gain speed or reduce delay, but to ease the load on the engine ; neither speed nor time concerned him, indeed he often afterwards recalled that not once on that never-to-be-forgotten run did he consult his watch or glance at a station clock. The train cleared the summit and the gear came back until at 30 per cent he let it roll on down the five-mile drop into Grantham Station, the battle won.

When he pulled up, a relief set of enginemen mounted

the footplate with the jocular remark that they had ‘ Special orders through from London that your Highnesses were to be relieved immediately on arrival and released from duty until your return working.’

Neither Eldridge nor Clarke rose to the bait ; somehow none of their reactions to the achievement were what might have been expected. There was no excitement or elation at their success ; no jubilation ; just a complete weariness of it all that left both men utterly indifferent to everything. Except perhaps for a smouldering bitterness.

The ‘ Guv'nor ’ had driven them very hard. Had he driven them *too* hard ?

‘ What is our return working ? ’

‘ 562 up Fish : about a dozen box-wagons full o' mackerel.’

Eldridge made no reply, but opening the firehole door drew Clarke's attention to the tubes.

‘ We've sprung the complete set ; she's leaking like a sieve ! And who can wonder ? ’

He sniffed the old familiar smell of burnt oil.

‘ Probably a couple of big ends hot as well – the oil isn't made that could keep a film over the crank-pins under loads like that. ’ We broke through it long since.

‘ Oh, well ! We'll work home with 562 and book Twenty-seven-Fifty “ Shed ” tomorrow. Give them a chance to go round her and put some of the damage right.

‘ Get your coat, Jack, we'll go over to the canteen.’

Jack got his coat and they went together, two very aged men.

Back on the platform, suitcase in hand, a passenger walked hurriedly up to an impatiently waiting business colleague to be greeted with :

'You're nearly forty minutes late, old man, rather annoying you know, they'll be waiting dinner.'

'Not my fault, blame the beastly train, a disgraceful journey, jog-trot all the way and I'll swear just now we weren't going faster than walking pace. I don't know what the railways are coming to. Bet if you could have seen the lazy blighters on the engine they'd have been sitting back smoking cigarettes.'

'Probably, we're certainly miles behind other countries when it comes to running trains. Look at Germany now, they know how to do things out there, streamlined *Flying Hamburgers* and the rest of it ; trouble is our chaps aren't interested in their jobs.'

'Exactly ! Time somebody woke. . . .'

They passed on through the barrier.

Chapter VIII

THE PRICE OF IT

' 562 Up ' terminated at King's Cross Goods Yard and when Driver Eldridge was relieved on arrival he handed in a formidable list of items to be entered on the Repairs Report Sheets when Twenty-seven-Fifty should reach Shed and be booked off.

' All tubes leaking firebox end.
Brick arch partly down.
Smoke-box door burnt and drawing air.
Superheater elements blowing in header.
All connecting rod big ends been overheated.
Connecting rod small ends to examine.
Both outside pistons blowing through.
Piston and spindle packing blowing badly.
Slide bar bolts loosened.
Axle-box wedges down.
Middle big end knocking.
Left side bottom main steam-pipe-joint strained.'

And there was certainly little enough of glory about 2750 as she was unhooked from the train and set back through the crossover *en route* to the loco. inlet signal. Nothing in the way of repairs had been done at Grantham where, at Eldridge's own request, they had been left to be dealt with at the London end, and the scars of her grim struggle with Stoke Bank were everywhere apparent. The fire half-quenched with water leaking from tubes and stays ; the warped and still-glowing smoke-box door burnt by accumulated ash made incandescent by air drawn through gaps in the ring ; the ominous hiss of blowing steam-joints and the sand-bespattered spokes and tyres.

As her return in some such condition had been anticipated, arrangements had already been made to keep her in and book her ' Shed.' She would have a thorough examination and there would be a chance to make the repairs to be expected after her cruel overloading. They had cleared a path for her through the various processes by the time she left the maze of tracks in the goods yard and came slowly round the bend into the loco. yard.

Without stopping she ran straight on to the new seventy-foot ' Muntz ' articulated, three-point suspension turntable, turning being the first operation carried out at the depot. These tables were an immense advance on the older ' balanced ' type which necessitated setting the engine carefully so that all the load was balanced on the centre pedestal. With the three-point suspension type the race rails carried the load and the position of the engine on the girders was less important. Moreover, they were always power-operated ; a little $\frac{3}{8}$ h.p. oscillating-cylinder air engine, powered by the vacuum brake on the locomotive, could turn the heaviest engine right round in less than ninety seconds.

Coming on with 18 inches of vacuum, the relief fireman quickly coupled the engine flexible hose connection with that of the tractor and proceeded to withdraw the table-locking bolts.

Calling ' Right ' to the relief driver, who opened the

On the turntable

large ejector to maintain the vacuum, the fireman started the tractor engine and 2750 swung gracefully round. He re-set the locking bars, disconnected the hose, and in response to his raised arm the engine was moved steadily off the turntable with a noticeable absence of the familiar thump that occurs as each pair of wheels changes table for stock rail on a balanced type.

Off the turntable and forward to the next operation, re-fuelling, but first a halt of fifteen minutes for a steam test which must be carried out while there is still a sufficient head for the purpose.

Knowing from his report of repairs required that Eldridge suspected broken piston-rings, the examining fitter tested these first as being the biggest job for the repair staff and requiring most steam. Taking each of the three pistons in turn, he set the right-hand crank on the back centre, in line with the connecting rod, and put the reversing lever in the mid-gear position. Keeping the brakes hard on, he then opened the regulator and a blow of steam up through the chimney indicated at once that it was leaking past the right-hand piston and that consequently the rings were, in fact, broken. Making an entry to this effect in his little, and very greasy, notebook he proceeded to test the middle piston in a similar manner, except that for this and for the left outside piston he put the lever in the 40 per cent back and fore gear positions respectively. Both were tight, and his attention was turned to the injectors. These he tested by opening the steam stop-cocks to various positions and noting that both injectors picked up the water quickly and cleanly.

Followed tests of the vacuum brake system and the

water-gauges, remaining steam and water cocks and the glands of the piston and valve-spindles, then up to the front end for an examination inside the smoke-box. Main steam and vacuum exhaust pipe joints ; blower ring and cock, and finally the extent and position of the air leak through the door itself.

A refresher at the coal stage and water column

The examination completed, and the list of repairs required swollen as a consequence, 2750 was released and taken forward to the mechanical coaling plant to receive six tons of best selected hard Yorkshire steam coal fed to her tender by a caterpillar feeder belt, one of four situated under the outlets from the overhead hopper. This was of 500 tons capacity, sufficient to supply the coal demands of the depot for twenty-four hours, and was charged by a wagon hoist ; full 20-ton wagons being taken up on a runway outside the plant, tipped into the hoppers and brought down again empty, the whole operation not exceeding four-and-a-half minutes. At intervals the coaling was stopped for a few minutes while coal trimmers went into the tender to break up excessively large blocks and to spread the delivery more or less evenly, so that heaping was avoided and the risk of a lump being thrown off reduced. This can be dangerous when a train is running through a station platform at 80 mph.

With tender well stacked and the weight of coal put on automatically recorded on the ribbon, the engine, still in the hands of its Moving Up set of enginemen, passed forward again to the jib water crane beside the coaling plant to receive 5000 gallons of lime-soda treated water delivered through ten-inch mains at a rate of over 1,000 gallons a minute. Then on to the next operation in the disposal line, the clearing of the firebox and smoke-box of their coal and ash residue respectively.

This was carried out over the disposal pits proper ; excavations 3 feet 6 inches deep extending some 200 feet between the rails. Here the engine was taken in hand by the firedroppers, a sturdy body of men, of fine physique, for the work is heavy and payment by piecework. One of their number mounted the footplate with a twelve-foot handled shovel, and opening the firehole door pushed all the live fire remaining on the grate forward to the middle front, where is situated the drop grate, a hinged section which may be lowered by means of a screw-operated system of links and levers provided for the purpose, causing the fire to drop through the opening so formed into the ashpan below, leaving the grate quite clean.

Re-setting the drop section to its ' up ' position, he left the footplate to descend into the pit and deal with the ashpan. First he quenched the fire by directing a jet of water through the front damper door with one of the short hose-pipes fitted at intervals along the pit sides. Then, with eyes shielded from dust by goggles, and hands protected from burning by leather gauntlets, he raked the clinker out of the ashpan through the door on to the floor of the pit, to be lifted out later on by ash-pit men who would load it into wagons for sale or for use as filling ballast.

Fire-grate and ashpan cleared, he went forward to the front of the engine and opened the smoke-box door, to be met on this occasion by a cloud of fine ash as the wind caught an accumulation that reached almost to the top of the blastpipe. Ordinarily this ash would not exceed six inches or so in depth, but as a result of the punishment that the engine had received and the high rate at which it had been fired, his work at the front end had been trebled, and his temper sharpened in proportion. This ash being light, however, was cleared reasonably soon, and after wiping round the asbestos ring that formed the door joint, he signalled that his work on the unit was finished.

The Move Up sets of enginemen worked only between the turntable and the disposal pit and the set who had brought 2750 up had gone back for the next. It was therefore a Take Away set who came up with the little shunting pilot-engine, coupled on to her, since she no longer carried sufficient steam-pressure to move herself, and slowly pulled her off the disposal pit. With much puffing and snorting importance, the pigmy negotiated the giant through points and crossings to the Shed entrance and left her at last in her berth at the bottom end of Number Six Road Main Line Shed.

Here, and barely come to rest, the foreman fitter and boilersmith together attended, each accompanied by his charge-hand, and with a note of what ravage it would be their job during the next twelve hours to repair. Judiciously, with years of experience behind them, each assigned particular repair work to particular fitters and boilersmiths. Thus to Jackson was given the task of opening up the right-hand cylinder walls to see if they had been scored by a piece of broken ring ; of stripping the cylinder cocks where other pieces might have fallen and lodged, possibly causing the plug cocks to jam, and of re-assembling the various parts afterwards. This man was also instructed to put new rings, and if necessary, new springs, in the packing of the piston and spindle glands and pull up the slide bar bolts.

To Simmons fell the task of taking down all three connecting rods, re-bushing the large and small ends of the outside ones if found to be necessary and closing the split brasses of the middle ; to Franklin the task of remaking the left-hand main steam-pipe joint ; to another, adjustment of the axle-box wedges, and so on.

Similarly, after he had examined the tubes in the firebox and the superheater elements, the foreman boilersmith distributed amongst the best men on his staff the work of expanding both tubes and elements ; renewing the brick arch and straightening the smoke-box door.

All those repairs, during the time they were on duty, would be personally and closely supervised by each of the foremen concerned, for the standard of maintenance at the depot stood high, and Driver Eldridge was well liked.

This work put in hand, the engine was taken over by the firebox-cleaners and tube-sweepers, the former with their small, key-shaped scrapers clearing crows' nests from round the projecting beadings of the tubes and encrusted ash from where it had stuck to the torpedo ends of the superheater elements ; sweeping down with their wire brushes the heads of the roof stay-bolts in the firebox crown, sheet, replacing with new ones the many firebars that the intense heat had in places fused together into a solid mass of shapeless iron. The tube-sweepers, working from the smoke-box end, passing a long, thin steel rod with a short length of springy hemp rope threaded through an eye at the end, down each separate tube in turn, sweeping out the soot and ash that, if left, would reduce the amount of heat passing through to the water side.

The boilerwashers, too, begin work now, a pair of men wearing protective clothing in the form of oilskin suits, leather gauntlets and wooden-soled clogs.

Through an armoured flexible hose-pipe they connect the blow-down cock of the engine to the blow-back line of the washing-out plant and, opening the cocks, allow what steam pressure still remains in the boiler to empty it of water by blowing this back into the plant tank. Next they connect another and lighter armoured hose to the wash-out pipe line, which carries water under a pressure of eighty pounds to the square inch, and using nozzles of various lengths, some straight and others bent, which they insert into wash-out plug holes situated at the front end of the barrel and round the firebox, wash off the scale and sludge from the water side of the tubes and plates with the powerful jet, a process that goes on for the best part of an hour. At the end of it the dislodged dirt is given a final sluice back towards the fire-box to settle on top of the foundation ring and be scraped out through the mud doors and taken away in wheelbarrows. Boiler cleaned, their final operation is to fill it up again, a reversal of the first operation, except that this time the connection is made from the boiler to the fill-up line of the washing-out plant, and charged with chemically softened water at nearly boiling point, leaving the boiler filled with hot water, from which steam could be raised, if required, in a matter of two hours.

With the boilerwashers, whose trailing pipes and flooding water prevent almost everybody else from working on the engine, out of the way, 2750, beginning to feel a little better, is taken in hand by a squad of four cleaners, each armed with his tin container holding oil-soaked sponge-cloths or swabs ; about two pints of cleaning oil ; a little composition and petroleum jelly for getting surface finish, and a supply of brick-dust and emery-cloth for brightening brass and steel respectively.

Short ladders with hooked staves are hung from the handrails to enable the boiler plates to be reached, and platforms rigged up on trestles for tender sides as two of the squad, one on each side, hurry to get the boiler and smoke-box cleaned while they are still hot, a condition that makes the task much easier and the finished surfaces brighter. The other two are busy with the wheels and 'motion' – the 'underneath,' swabbing off the grease first with their oil-soaked swabs and wiping down afterwards with dry, washed engine cloths. The springs and parts of the brake gear carry a thick layer of grease that has first to be scraped off with special scrapers, and for these parts too, a sharp-cutting kerosene has to be used, but after four hours of steady work under the vigilant eye of the foreman cleaner, the engine, except for finishing off the steel and brass, has been well-cleaned, and two hours more sees the tender clean also. Half an hour for the extra touches that mean so much to the final finish and the cleaners unhook their ladders, refill their containers, and begin operations elsewhere.

Observant of their progress has been the examining fitter, and when he sees that the underneath has been cleaned the better to reveal defects, missing split-pins, loose nuts, chafing pipes, cracks, flaws and very many other possible sources of trouble on the road, he takes his powerful acetylene handlamp, tyre gauges and hammer, and starts the most important and responsible work of giving the engine a close and careful examination to make quite sure that she is in perfectly sound and safe condition to run her 80 or 90 mph with the lives of her passengers depending perhaps, upon the discovery of a microscopic crack in a most inaccessible place.

Three lengths of the engine he traverses, in the form of the letter 'S'; front to back outside, back to front underneath in the pit – the middle bar of the 'S' – and finally, front to back again on the other side.

Buffers and drawgear; outside cylinder cock gear and piston packing; connecting rod small end, crosshead and slide bars; motion pins and fastenings; sand boxes and sand pipes ; brake hanger pins, blocks and cross-stay fastenings ; bogie and leading coupled wheels and tyres, the latter ‘ rung ’ with the hammer ; leading end of main frame ; side rod collar pins, set bolts and oil box screw tops ; leading end lubricator and anti-carboniser pipes ; footsteps ; mechanical lubricators, lids, pipes, driving gear and fastenings ; connecting rod big end ; driving wheel and tyre ; driving-wheel brake gear ; middle of main frame ; driving side rod and knuckle pin ; trailing coupled wheel, tyre and brake gear ; trailing end of main frame ; trailing side rod ; pony axle box and spring gear ; injector fastenings, pipes, clips and control rods ; cab handrails ; distance between engine and tender and condition of buffing-gear ; hand-brake fastenings ; leading tender spring gear ; axle-box ; horn stay ; keep ; frame ; brake gear ; steam-heating pipe and clip ; intermediate and trailing tender sections similarly, and then into the pit and examining from back to front, tender buffing and draw gear ; guard irons ; brake cross stays ; pull rods ; hangars and blocks ; wheels and tyres ; vacuum brake and steam heating pipe lines, clips and connections ; brake adjusting screw, rods, shaft and cylinders ; draw-gear and flexible connections between engine and tender ; engine pony wheels and tyres ; coupled wheel springs and spring gear ; coupled wheel axle-boxes and lubricating pipes ; damper gear ; brake cross-stays ; middle big end ; middle small end, crosshead and slidebar ; middle piston packing ; middle cylinder cock gear ; vacuum brake cylinders ; pipes, clips and connections ; bogie spring gear, centre pedestal and frames.

And then out of the pit to examine the other side in the same way.

During this gruelling test the examining fitter has noted in his book many items that will have to be given attention before 2750 takes the road again and, his examination complete, he reports these to the foreman fitter, who assigns the consequent work involved in dealing with them to trained men of known reliability, after himself inspecting the progress made with the heavier booked repairs, so that all the work remaining to be done on the engine may be properly co-ordinated.

And those tubes ' leaking like a sieve ' at Grantham ?

Drum-tight now, re-expanded into the tube-plate by the latest ' Wageor ' equipment ; an electrically driven horizontal shaft carrying the tube-expander in a socket at the end, which the tuber inserts into each of the tubes in turn, expanding them to a tight fit in the hole of the tube-plate.

Working at the rate of two hundred to the hour, the motor clicks in and clicks out as the pressure on the wall of each tube end reaches the required amount and a shift on to the next is made. Soon that operation, too, will be completed and the new brick arch built up, extending six feet back from the tube-plate towards the firehole door, each quarry carefully examined for trace of splitting or over-baked clay.

At the front end new rings have been fitted to the right-hand piston-head and the front cylinder-cover is being replaced, opposite nuts of the studs that secure it pulled up in turn so that an even bearing will be obtained on the copper joint ring all round. Fresh piston rod and spindle packing has been put into the stuffing boxes ; slide bar bolts tightened up ; the nuts re-pinned and the middle big end brasses let together, linered up and re-assembled.

Foreman fitter and foreman boilersmith both were at the engine when, towards four o'clock in the afternoon, the running foreman on duty in the course of his progress round the shed to see what engines were available to work the trains, came and put his inevitable question, ' When can I have her ? ' Then followed the equally inevitable argument in which the pressing demands for Pacific power were urged on the one hand and on the other the absolute necessity for sufficient time in which to complete the repairs thoroughly ; it ended, as such arguments always did, in the compromise that exemplified mutual goodwill and team work, which contributed so much to the high standard of the depot.

' You can have her by seven o'clock.'

' Need running in ? '

' She should need it – with new bushes, packings and rings on the right outside. What's Eldridge tomorrow ? '

' Ten-fifty ; fairly light loading, but a bit fast in places for a first trip.'

I'd rather chance her on that with Eldridge than on a ' Parly ' in the hands of anyone else. I'll O.K. her for the ten-fifty, provided he works it.'

And the running foreman continued on his survey, later to give instructions for 2750 to be lit up for that train.

This resulted at about 4 a.m. the next day in the appearance on her footplate of a steam-raiser with his three wood-stick-and-shaving firelighters.

After spreading some medium-sized coal thinly over the fire-grate, he cleared a small space in the middle, but not quite down to the bars, so that lighted shavings could fall among and intermix with what remained. Taking his firelighters he lowered them with a firing shovel on to the cleared space thus formed and lightly covered them with selected small coal.

Having tested the water-gauges and satisfied himself that the boiler carried a good half-glass, also that the damper was fully open, he lighted a few pieces of oily cleaning-cloth on the blade of the shovel and tipped them dexterously on to the little mound that he had formed. Quickly the firelighters ignited, and when they were well burning he placed more small coal on the heap, closed the firehole door to obtain the maximum possible draught through, and not over, his fire, opened the blower valve, and left the footplate, to return every half-hour or so, stir the fire with a ' pricker ' add more coal and keep a watch on the water-level.

Shortly after seven o'clock his skill and industry were rewarded by the sound of a low, continuous whistle. Although no steam pressure was as yet registered on the gauge, it was beginning to build up ; there was sufficient to leak past the valve of the whistle and set this into vibration, but not enough to keep it tight up on its seating. At 5 lb. to the square inch the whistling ceased and the blower began to function, creating a little draught on the fire, the effect of which quickly became apparent, for in another thirty minutes the gauge needle had climbed to 20 lb., in the next to 45 lb. and thereafter its movement over the scale was steady until, at half-past eight, it stood on the 200 line and had to be checked from mounting still higher by putting on one of the injectors, both as a means of using some of the steam and of cooling the water in the boiler sufficiently to hold the needle stationary.

Still the steam-raiser kept 2750 under his observation, for it remained his responsibility so far as steam, fire and water were concerned, until the enginemen should appear to prepare her for the day's service. But it is not very long before they do so, and with a critical eye for his performance, Fireman Clarke assumes command much as the master of a liner takes over from the pilot, while Eldridge, a little more generous even than usual in the application of his oil-feeder to newly fitted parts, brightens as he notes the work that has been put into the engine, the care and craftsmanship with which it has been carried out, and the obvious fettle and shape of his 2750, restored once more.

In a little over an hour there is a short whistle up, the hiss of steam from open cylinder-cocks, a shouted ' You're clear ' and she moves slowly away, soon to be thundering north again at 90 mph, 500 tons behind her, and only a ribbon of steel ahead.

Chapter IX

THE BLOWN FUSIBLE PLUG

Enginemen, like policemen, postmen and pressmen, are men for whom there is no regular train to work in the morning and regular train home again in the evening. Armchairs and slippers are just as frequently available to them as to everybody else, but they are as likely to be enjoyed at eleven o'clock in the morning as at eleven o'clock at night.

It takes many years to grow accustomed to this departure from nature's dictum that we work by day and sleep at night, but sticking to the golden rule ' Get up to go to work ' does the trick in the end and then the irregular hours of duty that are the lot of enginemen have their advantages. Not only is it often convenient to be free for an entire morning or afternoon, when other folk are prisoners of desk or bench, but night work can offer experiences and interests never felt or known by sleeping humanity. Among these is the ineffable glory of a late June sunrise ; such a dawn as opened up the sky one morning when 2750, bringing in the *Night Scotsman* reached the last lap of her journey passing Hatfield ; a downhill run home, a full head of steam and an inch of water in the glass. Clarke, conscious of all these good things, comfortably resting on his bucket seat ; planning a drop more water ' in a minute or two ' but little more shovel work ; Eldridge, conscious, too, of the peace of the hour, the outline of the countryside limned sharply against a pale green, flame-shot cloudless sky ; not a sound anywhere save the soft purring of his engine.

Running fast and well with time in hand, it seemed to him, despite the attraction of his comfortable bed, good to be astir that morning, breathing in the cool sharp air and then —!

' Hold her ! '

Quick as Clarke had been, Eldridge was as quick and had seen the same thing at the same time.

Hadley Wood Inner Home signal flung up to the danger position in his face !

' Steady ! Must keep my head. Brake first ! '

He pulled the handle down hard. Air rushed direct into every brake-cylinder throughout the train and brought the brake-blocks into screaming grip with every wheel.

' Next the regulator,' he thought, and slammed it shut on the instant.

' Now to reverse. . . . But no ! ' Clarke was young. No knowing what he might do. Might jump and get smashed to pulp against the buttress of Headley Road Bridge.

He glanced across at the footplate to see his mate's white, frightened face turned towards him. On it was the question ' What shall I do ? ' – the appeal of youth to age and experience in a moment of terror, brave enough to jump if told to jump, ready enough to stay if told to stay, asking only to be told which.

' Wait for it ! '

Eldridge began to pull up the lever while his mind darted this way and that as he wondered what would happen when they got round the curve ahead.

' It may be a spread of derailed wagons off one of the

night freights,' he thought. ' If so, there's a chance we'll cut clean through it.' He turned to the speed indicator. 73 mph !

At that speed the train with its 150 tons of steel on the front was like an arrow tipped with lead, shot from a gigantic bow. It would cut through practically anything – anything except another locomotive. ' If there's an engine mixed up with it,' he thought, ' and a big engine, what will happen to us then ? We'll hit and the front will go up. Always the front goes up. Some-times she falls to left and sometimes to right. Either way we may be thrown clear, but if she topples backwards on us we're crushed and done for ! '

He looked at the half-open firehole door and motioned Clarke to shut it. Bad enough to be pinned down until the doctors amputate, without being roasted while waiting.

' Well ! What's round that curve ? ' It seemed to Eldridge a curve that had no straight beyond it, as with whistle blaring 2750 plunged on.

What use are brakes when you're running at 73 mph and downhill at that ? They had been hard on for what seemed to him a full three minutes, yet as he looked again at the indicator he saw that they were still travelling at 58.

Would they never get round ?

Yes ! They were round, and the straight lay ahead, ten miles of it, and every yard as clear as on the day they laid it, and – gladder sight even that that ! – green lights as far as the eye could see : New Barnet Distant, Home, and Starter ; Oakleigh Park Distant ; even the greens of the New Southgate section could be seen in the distance.

A little in front, on the up local line, a suburban tank engine chugged its workmen's train manfully along towards the station, and way ahead on the down main line could be seen the express headlights of the first paper train out of London.

For the rest, the scene was just as it had been but a few seconds before, the flame in the sky deepening to blood red, the last of the stars fading its way out and over all the tranquillity and stillness of a perfect summer dawn.

Slower in his reaction to obvious safety than in his reaction to imminent danger, Eldridge made no movement for countable seconds, and then instinctively released the red hot brake blocks from smoking tyres and let the train run on. Some minutes passed before he opened the regulator again, and when he did so, it was to half-quadrant only. Badly shaken, he sat very still.

' What was it ? '

Eldridge pointed through the cab window to the green lights ahead.

' I don't know. It may have been that the signalman mis-judged our speed, possibly new to the box, or maybe a relief man ; thought we should be clear of his Inner Home so he set it back to the ON position. An easy enough mistake to make.'

Clarke too, sat very still.

Until his eye caught the gauge glass with just a trace of the water level, but no more, less than half an inch above the nut. He got quickly to his feet and put on the live steam injector ; the exhaust steam injector had been on throughout the trip. ' Cut that fine enough ! ' he thought as he opened the firehole door for the final fire-up of the day.

But, shovel in hand, he stopped at sight of a fire-bed such as he had never seen before, nor, as his staff record card ultimately bore witness, was ever to see again.

Midway between the backplate and the edge of the brick arch, central between the two firebox sides, lay a

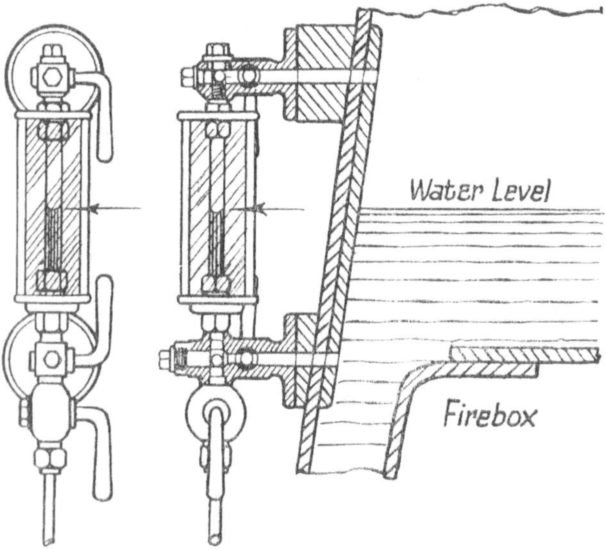

The water level gauge

round black patch, perhaps three feet in diameter, and across the full width of the box for a foot back from the throat plate stretched a black band, both of them the black of dead fire. So dead that he could discern the grey streaks of ash intermixed with charred, unburnt coal. Over all was fog-like steam rising from the fire-bed and the ominous hiss of the age-long battle between fire and water.

With his expression changing from amazement to consternation as realisation of what had happened came slowly to him, he dug his shovel back under the coal on the shovelling plate and, getting down on his knees, looked upward through the firehole door to the firebox crown sheet. There he saw two solid jets of water issuing from the holes of the front and back fusible plugs. The first, striking the brick-arch and running down and off the front and through the ash openings, had blackened the fire across the throat plate, the second flooded directly down to the centre of the black circle between the firehole door and the arch.

Clarke turned to look at Eldridge, and for a moment knew the fear of a justly aroused anger, the fear of the small boy caught in the jam cupboard, of the man who doubles round the wrong corner to face a uniform and outstretched arms. More even than a physical fear, the fear that as a consequence of his carelessness all the comradeship and goodwill built up in the years of their working together must inevitably go to pieces. No more would he be ‘ mate ’ to, and feel the kindliness of, this fine man whom he respected so much and liked so well.

That official censure would mean three days’ – and perhaps a week’s – suspension from duty meant nothing at all to him ; but that, through himself, his driver would receive the same punishment, cut him deeply. Worst of all would be the ineradicable entry on the staff record of both men, there until the day they left the service of the Company ; in his mate’s case a clean white card with three years left to run, now to be smeared because of himself, with the ugly mark – ‘. . . allowed your engine to become short of water so that two fusible plugs were melted, and it became a total failure on the road.'

With the abandonment of despair he got to his feet again and touched Eldridge on the shoulder.

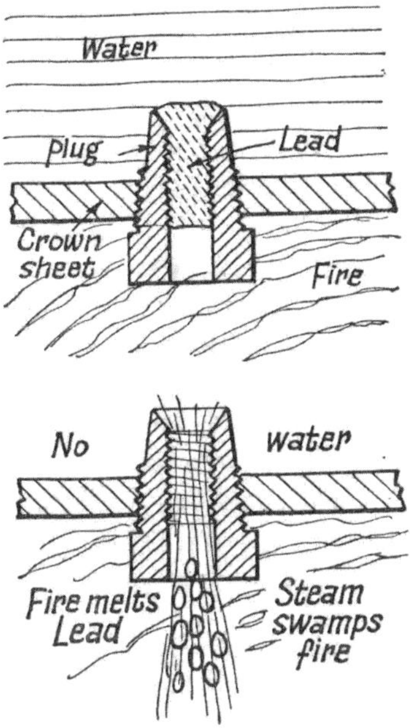

Sectional view of the fusible plug in action

' Look at the fire.'

Eldridge, after glancing at his signals, turned to the firehole door and knew instantly.

' Fool ! you've blown a plug.'

' Two,' replied Clarke with that inanity which sometimes masks deep feeling.

Eldridge's shoulders squared as he drew himself up ;

his neck swelled and his fists clenched as his anger rose and sought outlet in physical violence. But he was too well-trained to lose control of himself. Had they been off the footplate, for all his sixty-two years, he would have punished Clarke in the primitive, elemental way that alone satisfies a man and it is more than likely that he would be the better for it afterwards. But to attempt such a thing on the footplate was unthinkable and without a word further he went back to his seat, shoulders sagging again and head maybe a little lower than was usual with him.

Clarke followed him across.

' I'm sorry mate.' It sounded feeble enough, but was all he could bring himself to say.

Perhaps it was the helplessness and hopelessness of the way in which the words were spoken that recalled to Eldridge the sterling character and high ability of this hot-tempered, hare-brained young fireman of his, whom he had trained so successfully, and steadied so often. At any rate, the flare of his anger passed in the face of this second emergency.

He glanced first at both water-gauges and saw the bare inch of water, then he tested them, opening and closing the drain cocks, noting the fall and rise again of the water-level to become still in both glasses at exactly the same height.

No fault there. He might know there would be no fault with the gauges of 2750.

A look upwards to the pressure-gauge showed him he had 180 lb. of pressure ; already the damping out of the fire had pulled the needle back, but he was passing Wood Green now and might possibly get the train through.

He decided to try.

' Fire small stuff lightly to the bright parts only,' he said and opened the regulator to full quadrant.

Only too ready to atone in any way he could, Clarke did as he was bid.

' Now clear the dead fire off the bars under the back plug ; let the water run straight through into the ashpan.'

This took a little longer, needing a good deal of skilful manipulation with the slice, but a bare place was cleared, the needle stood at 150 lb. and the signals of Harringay came into view.

Eldridge himself shut the cock of the live steam injector. He must conserve every pound of steam. Opening the blower-cock, he pulled up the gear to 10 per cent. The needle was back to 130 lb, but on the down grade home he would get there if no signal checks intervened. His major concern was that the pressure would fall to a point where he would be unable to keep the brakes off. Already he was compelled to use the large ejector from time to time in order to do so.

But no signal checks did intervene and he was able to keep the brakes off so that none could tell there was anything wrong with the engine when she brought the train gracefully to a stand against the buffer stops of Number One Arrival Platform.

Leaving the footplate at once he walked quickly over to the inspector's office.

' In a bit of trouble, George. If I'm to get to the shed under my own steam you must get me off the train and away inside ten minutes.'

The inspector got up from his chair at once ; reading

much in the expression of his old friend. He asked no questions whatsoever.

' As soon as we've got the luggage out I'll have the pilot on the back and draw down the coaches clear of the crossover. You set back through that and drop down to the signal. I'll ask Jim to get you the road. When you've gone we'll put the cars back and carry on. O.K. ? '

' Thanks, mate,' said Eldridge, and returned to the footplate to carry out the arranged movements in less than eight minutes.

With barely a hundred pounds of steam 2750 crept slowly into the Loco. Yard, there to have the fire thrown out immediately. At least he had been spared the ignominy of being towed in behind a shunting engine, the thing that he dreaded above all others.

He turned to Clarke : ' I'm reporting this personally to the Guv'nor when he comes. Will you be here at nine o'clock and come in with me ? '

' Yes,' replied Clarke, and with no further word the two men parted.

And at nine o'clock, as the District Loco Superintendent turned the handle of his office door, his two crack enginemen, now washed, changed and breakfasted, approached him.

' Can I have a few minutes with you, sir ? ' said Eldridge.

' Certainly,' was the reply, though raised eyebrows revealed the unexpectedness of the request.

The three entered the office together and Smedley, sweeping aside a pile of correspondence, sat down at his desk, motioning the other two to draw up chairs.

' I very much regret to report, sir, that we have dropped the fusible plugs on Twenty-seven-Fifty.'

Instantly the face of their chief changed. It took on a severity unusual to the two who faced him. He said coldly :

' From you, Eldridge, that is an incredible statement to hear.'

' I'm afraid it is true, sir.'

' I suggest you explain.'

' There's little enough to say ; we were working the up *Night Scotsman* and had had an uneventful run as far as Hadley Wood. There we had the Inner Home thrown up in front of us and had to check severely. A few minutes afterwards Clarke here went to fire up and called my attention to a black fire. The front and back plugs had dropped. I managed to get through and up to the shed, and then took my first opportunity of reporting personally to you.'

Smedley turned to Clarke.

' What have you to say ? '

' Only that I didn't let the water down that low, I'm prepared to swear it.'

' Evasion is unlike you, Clarke,' said Smedley, the frown on his face deepening.

' I'm not evading, sir.'

' Were the plugs blown or not ? ' snapped Smedley.

' They were blown, sir.'

' Have you ever known or heard of a fusible plug being blown without the boiler being short of water ? '

' No, sir.'

' Then clearly you let the level drop ; don't beat about the bush.'

To this Clarke made no reply and Smedley continued : ' Where were you, do you think, when they went ? '

'I know they were all right at Hatfield, because I had fired up not long before and taken a general look round, thinking I had little more to do as we were on time, with a full head of steam, and' – he hesitated a second – 'sufficient water.'

'How much water?'

Clarke hesitated again, then said, 'an inch.'

Smedley, and Eldridge too, for that matter, sat forward on hearing this.

'Only an inch! Is it your usual practice to run with only an inch of water in the glass?'

'No, sir.'

'Then why on this occasion?'

'We were running well. I'd nothing to worry about; I knew more water was wanted in the boiler, and intended to open the live steam-injector in a minute or two, but in that interval the check came that my mate told you about.'

'And it so scared you that you forgot all about your water level – a fireman's greatest responsibility?'

'It did scare me I admit, sir, but I didn't forget the water, and when I did put on the injector after we got going again there was still nearly half an inch above the bottom nut.'

'I see, so like that, the water was never out of the glass?'

'Couldn't have been.'

'Then how came the plugs to drop?'

'I don't know, sir.'

'Clarke, you're lying!'

Clarke's face suffused to a dull red, but he kept both his temper and his respect for his superior as he replied:

' No, sir, I'm not.'

Here Eldridge interposed.

' That check gave both of us a nasty shock ; I think perhaps in the confusion and alarm my mate forgot the water. Such a thing has never even nearly occurred before, and in spite of it I have the fullest confidence in him. I don't want to lose him, sir. We'll both take our punishment for this, but leave him with me and I'll promise you it will never occur again.'

Clarke sat as if carved in wood ; he made no move and gave no sign that he had heard his driver's appeal, but he remembered it for many years after that eventful interview.

' It's a question of competence, Eldridge. No fireman who lets a boiler get short of water is competent to handle the big stuff that we have to handle.'

He paused. ' Yet there's something out of character here.'

He turned to Clarke : ' I refer to yours, which I know a good deal better than you may suppose. I know you to be a hot-tempered young trouble-maker, always mixed up in any mischief that's about, the plague of half the supervisors at the depot – but you are not a liar. Now, listen, Clarke. Did you or did you not let the water out of the glass of this engine ? '

Clarke, eyes steady on those of his questioner, answered :

' I did not, sir.'

' Very well then, in spite of the clear evidence to the contrary, I accept your statement. I have greater faith in my own judgement of a man's character than in the evidence of my own eyes.'

The District Locomotive Superintendent then said : ' Having disposed of that, we are still left with no explanation as to how the plugs came to be dropped. Can either of you, without any suggestion of cross-questioning or blame, help me to get to the bottom of that mystery ? '

Neither man spoke for a while, then Eldridge said diffidently, for he had far less confidence in his mate's truthfulness than the other had, and no doubt whatever in his own mind that Clarke had misjudged the water-level.

' Could it be anything to do with that signal business, sir ? '

She was all right before and all wrong afterwards.'

Smedley smiled.

' Not unless the arm jumped down from the post, slipped into the firebox when you were not looking, drilled out the plugs and jumped back again.' He thought for a moment. ' And yet . . . . I wonder.'

He sat suddenly forward in his chair.

' What were you doing when you applied the brakes ? ' he snapped.

' Seventy-three, sir. I looked at the indicator to see our chances of stopping.'

' And what did you get down to ? '

' Fifty-five or so.'

' How long were the brakes on, do you think ? '

' About three minutes.'

' More likely two,' Smedley murmured to himself, ' even so, from seventy-three to fifty-five is a stiff retardation. It might do it.'

He spoke again to Eldridge.

' I think we're getting on to the track of it, but I must

know as accurately as possible how long those brakes were on. Now I want you, Eldridge, to go over your movements again here. Turn your chair away from me, put your hand up as if it were on the brake handle and make the emergency application movement. Then let your mind go over the whole incident, seeing what you saw then, and feeling what you felt then. When you consider the same interval of time has passed lift your hand again as you did when you released the brakes.'

He reached down to a drawer of his desk and brought out a stop watch.

' Clarke, you go into the next office for a few minutes, I shall want you to check him.'

Not quite understanding, but anxious to be of all the help he could, Eldridge turned away from his chief, the better to concentrate on his mental recapitulation, and after a few seconds brought his hand down smartly in a downward movement. At the same moment Smedley pressed the spring of his stop watch. An interval of intense interest for Smedley followed as the passing of each second went towards confirming his idea of a possible cause, and then Eldridge's hand was lifted again to indicate that he had released the brakes, and the watch was stopped.

' Two minutes and five seconds ; not long, but with half an inch only, long enough. Now get Clarke back.'

Clarke's estimate was longer, two minutes nineteen seconds, which perhaps revealed his greater mental turmoil during that nerve-racking experience ; but striking an average, or even at two minutes with a firebox temperature of more than 2,000° Fahrenheit, Smedley was satisfied that he had arrived at the cause – quite satisfied.

He sat back in his chair.

'Well, Eldridge, and you too, Clarke, in the whole course of my career I have never been more glad than I am at this moment in being able to tell you that you are both cleared of all responsibility in connection with the dropping of these fusible plugs on 2750.'

This announcement was met with the silence of incomprehension until at last Eldridge spoke :

'Do you mean that we didn't drop them, sir ?'

'I do. You had nothing whatever to do with it.'

'But they were dropped, but by reason of a unique set of circumstances, over which you had no control. I'll explain.'

He picked up the glass pencil tray that lay on the table and, emptying out the pencils, placed a slab of indiarubber at one end. Taking the tray over to the hand basin he ran just sufficient water into it to cover the rubber, then replaced the tray on the table.

'Imagine that to be the boiler of your engine with the top sliced off exposing the crown sheet of the firebox as represented by the top surface of the indiarubber. It is, you see, covered with water, not much water, but still no harm would be done while there is any at all. Now your boiler was travelling at seventy-three miles an hour when suddenly you applied the brakes and reduced its speed to fifty-five. Watch the top surface of the rubber when I reproduce that sudden retardation.'

He drew the tray sharply along the top of the table, then stopped it. The water surged forward, splashing over the front end and leaving nearly the whole of the rubber uncovered at the rear end.

'The crown sheet of your firebox was uncovered, just

as that rubber was, for nearly two minutes, quite long enough for the intense heat of the fire under it to melt the lead out of the plugs. As the water surged back again and steadied down there were two neat holes for it to stream through down onto the fire.

When on the Suburbans, Eldridge, travelling chimney first, didn't you sometimes get a violent blowing through the safety valves when you pulled up at a station ? '

' Very often.'

' The same cause, but to a less extent ; the water goes forward off the crown sheet, but in such cases the time is too short before it is back again for any damage to be done.'

' Does this mean then, sir, that there will be no entries on the record cards ? '

' Certainly it does. I should be justified in recording the prompt action of both of you in the face of an emergency, but if you take my advice you won't ask for it. The best card of all is a perfectly blank card without entry of any kind, good or bad.'

He smiled up at them. ' Now bundle off out of my office and let me get on with my work.'

His eye had already caught sight of a telegram on the table with the words : ' Short supply of coal send five wagons all speed.'

' And tell Jackson to ring your tyres. If you've had them hot enough, they'll be loosened.'

Outside the office door, the two men stood for a moment in silence then, by mutual impulse, grasped hands.

' Well, that's over ! ' ejaculated Clarke in relief, as they separated and each made for home and the morning paper.

CHAPTER X

BREAKING FOR THE HUNDRED

THROUGH the months of summer and early autumn 2750 ran on ; always in the hands of her inseparable partners, steadily enhancing a reputation for performance and reliability that had grown beyond all precedent.

She had become renowned not only at her home depot, where ' Might be on '50 '—' Think we've got '50 ' were common expressions of satisfaction, but right down to, and even over, the Border, for among ' Loco.' men the good, bad or indifferent, be it of design or behaviour, type or unit, is argued at length, and once the verdict has been given, it travels with the trains, far and wide.

Consequently Eldridge, master of the machine and aware of its capabilities, was entirely unperturbed when told by the clerk of the signing-on office that he was wanted by the ' Guv'nor ' ; it was believed for ' some special job.'

' Well, Eldridge,' said his chief with a smile as the clean-overalled driver stood fresh and alert before his desk, ' blown any more fusible plugs yet ? '

' No, sir ; nor shall, I hope. My mate is still looking for that Hadley Wood signalman.'

' It is to be hoped he has no dependants ! Tell me, Eldridge, in what sort of fettle is Twenty-seven-Fifty these days ? '

' Same as she always has been, sir, the freest steaming and best running engine on the road ! '

‘ Good. I’ve something a little out of the ordinary for the three of you that I’m anxious should be carried off without any hitch. Anything that even looked like a failure or a ‘ flop ’ as the young people call it these days, would lose us one of the best opportunities that has ever come our way to show folk what we can do.’

The propeller-driven Kruckenburg Car (1931)

‘ We shan’t let you down, sir,’ replied Eldridge with complete confidence.

‘ I know. That’s why you are here now. They want us to run rather an unusual special train, King’s Cross to Leeds and back. Actually it is a trial trip. The results of it will very likely settle whether or not it would be possible to operate regularly in this country an altogether new form of train service. There has recently sprung into existence, first in Germany and now in the United States, a type of locomotive that is a complete breakaway from what we know as a locomotive here. It is driven by an internal combustion engine, like a super-powerful motor bus.

In the German machine this engine drives an enormous airscrew or aeroplane propeller on a single railcar, and I am told it has reached a speed of one-hundred-and-forty-three miles an hour. The Americans apply it in a different way ; the diesel motor engine is made to drive a generator which supplies electric current to

The American Streamliner (Union Pacific 1934)

motors and these rotate the wheels. Such locomotives, diesel-electric they call them, are also running trains regularly at over a hundred miles an hour.'

' Isn't there any boiler ? '

' No, and so no coal or coal dust and dirt, no boiler-washing or steam-raising or tube-cleaning, in fact, for ninety-six per cent of the time they are actually in service, working trains, and that gives them a big pull over our steam locomotives, which are seldom more than eighty per cent of their time in traffic.'

'Do you think they will drive the steam locomotive off the road, sir?'

'The German idea, no. That's just a stunt; but the American diesel-electric I'm not so sure about. It has immense possibilities and America being an oil-producing country it's bound to develop there, and I think it will ultimately displace the steam locomotive. So far as this country's concerned, we are coal-producers and will use that fuel for as long as we can, but I doubt if we shall be able to prevent an invasion by the diesel-electric. We may both live to see some of our crack trains headed by that flat and uninteresting box of tricks. Over here I think the battle will be raged between the diesel-electric and the straight electric locomotive. And I shouldn't like to guess which will win the day. Either way, I'm afraid the steam locomotive is on the way out. In fifty years it will have gone.'

'A lot will be sorry to see that, sir.'

'Yes, Eldridge, but not so many as you may think. The dying process will be gradual and as new men come along they will be diesel – or electric-minded; people will get used to the new motive power unit and forget the old. But we're not passing out without a struggle and you will be taking an important part in it.'

'I'd like nothing better, sir.'

'It is proposed to see whether some of these spectacular speeds I have mentioned couldn't at least be *approached* by steam locomotives, given reasonable loads, of course. After all, nobody has ever yet tried to see how fast a steam-hauled train can run. The trend has always been to see how great a weight it can pull – the revenue-earning angle in fact. There is known to have been an occasion in 1904 when a train hauled by one of the Great Western four-coupled engines, the *City of Truro*, covered a quarter of a mile in 8.8 seconds, which represents a speed of 102.3 mph, but that, like the German railcar, was an isolated instance. Now our directors want to find out whether it would be possible to put in the timetables of the Company a lightly-loaded but very fast passenger-train service between London

G.W.R. 'City of Truro'

and Leeds, and if it is possible, the speed at which it could be booked to run.

'So we're going to have a trial run on Thursday next with a load of 220 tons ; and I want you, with Clarke, to work it, and to put up as good a performance as you can. On the results of it will be decided whether such 'High Speed Units,' as they would be called, are practicable, and, if they are, the running times that should be allowed over each section.

'Everything connected with the matter is highly confidential at this stage, and even I myself can't give you much information about it. There are rumours that to work such trains a new type of steam locomotive, and probably coaches as well, would be designed which would be streamlined in order to reduce wind resistance. But that is all conjecture !

There will be no passengers as such, on the train, but possibly some of the Company's high officers, and some technicians checking speeds, times, oscillation and so on. You must, of course, take every precaution to ensure the safe running of the train, but you are free to run – and run fast. I confess that I shall be very gratified if you do, in fact, touch the hundred-mile-an-hour mark, and hold it long enough to ensure no later dispute about it. But that will be entirely up to you.'

' We shan't disappoint you, sir. What about Calder Bridge ? '

' Pacifics are still not allowed to run over it, but it would be strengthened as part of the scheme. And meantime I expect you will be allowed over under a stiff speed restriction.'

' Shall I tell Clarke ? '

' As much as you think he'll need to know. We shall tune up the engine for the trip. What needs attention on her ? '

' There's never been much wrong with Twenty-seven-Fifty. I've nothing in particular to book.'

' How does she steam ? '

' Well. Perhaps you'll have the blast-pipe burnt out and re-aligned and the arch tested. I've no reason to suppose it's weak, but if part of it did collapse it would ruin the run.'

' Quite. We'll see to it and run over the setting of

the valves, too. Put a bit more on the lubricator feeds – you'll be supplied with a special high-speed oil – and retrim all bearings. I wish you the best of luck.'

Eldridge left the office feeling elated. Apart from a natural pride that he should have been chosen for this most important duty, he was immensely interested in its possibilities. A load of a mere 220 tons behind such an engine as 2750 or, for that matter, any other Pacific, was unprecedented, and he wondered how far his technique and driving experience would serve him in such altogether untried circumstances.

Consequently, as well as being keyed up and essentially ready, he was undecided so far as handling the engine was concerned when, a few minutes before 10.50 on a grey autumn Thursday morning, he set back out of Gas Works Tunnel and locked the buck-eye couplings of engine and train with a snap.

Very few people were on the platform, but those there were important, and some gathered round the locomotive, which for the occasion was perhaps even more resplendent than usual. Among these was Headquarters Inspector Bowles who, very officious in bowler hat and black mackintosh, soon elbowed his way through them and mounted the footplate to address the somewhat startled Eldridge with :

' Now, my man, I want a good run today. A lot depends upon my report of this trip ! '

Knowing him by sight – and repute – Eldridge made no reply, but when to this admonition the Inspector added :

' Drive on a full open regulator and cut off as necessary,' he could not resist replying very seriously :

' I shall. And stop at any signals which may be at danger.'

Not quite sure what to make of this, but giving Eldridge the benefit of the doubt the Inspector stepped across to the cab door to look, with hands on handrail pillars, benignly down upon those less fortunate people who could not aspire to share his eminence.

' That chap coming with us ? ' queried Clarke.

' Suppose so,' replied Eldridge. ' The Guv'nor said something about a headquarters inspector travelling, but it's hard luck it should be that one.'

' He may think so too before he gets back,' quoth Clarke darkly.

Eldridge drew from his pocket the sectional timing schedule of the train, carefully and cleanly copied out on to a thick piece of cardboard, and after a final glance round the cab which satisfied him that everything was in first-class order, set himself to the study of the first few sections, turning over in his mind where best to run as fast as he could, and where it would be policy in the long run to ease up a little. One thing he had decided upon as taking the best advantage of his light load : to accelerate and get into his stride as quickly as possible after the ' Right away ' signal was given. He aimed to be running in the seventies before he reached Wood Green.

Over no section anywhere was the schedule, with so light a load, anything like a possible minimum for 2750, but Eldridge, having wisely been made aware of the circumstances underlying the trial, intended to clip it wherever he could, and run both down and up trips in the shortest possible time. And a lot depended, he decided, on a rapid acceleration out of the station right at the start, and subsequent acceleration up to the 80's – higher if possible. With no fear of creating too fierce a draught (and so disturbing the fire-bed) to consider, he determined to reverse his usual technique and get the most power out of the engine while the resistance was there to use it on. He would run all out up the Bank to Potter's Bar, and get in hand all the time he could. Thereafter most of the tractive effort would be dissipated in overcoming the internal friction set up by the speed of the train.

These deliberations were somewhat roughly interrupted by the pressing need of Inspector Bowles to give his audience a further demonstration of his authority and importance. This time, addressing Clarke, he said :

' Fireman, just get busy with your slacker pipe and damp down some of the dust on the coal and the foot-boards : you won't have much opportunity once we get started.'

Without a word, Clarke took up the pipe and, opening his injector steam cock, played the jet of water over the coal on the tender. It was unfortunate that, taking a step backward in the process, he should have tripped over the bucket, because this made him drop the pipe in such a manner that the legs of Inspector Bowles, from the knees downward, received a jet of scalding hot water issuing full bore from a $\frac{3}{8}$ inch nozzle with some 200 lb. per square inch steam pressure behind it.

Almost as though he had anticipated some such misadventure, Eldridge had the injector shut off within a split second and, with a profusely apologetic Clarke, hastened to repair the damage by dabbing at the legs of the infuriated inspector with clean engine-cloths, but it was possibly as well that, before that aggrieved gentleman could become articulate, preliminary whistles sounded from the platform and the slamming of carriage doors brought all three men on the footplate to attention for the job in hand.

Driver Robert Eldridge was destined that day to break more than one of the Company's rules and regulations. The first was at the moment when he opened the regulator and started the train on its memorable journey. He opened the steam sand valve, being determined to lose neither speed nor seconds by wasteful slipping of wheels in unproductive work. As the train virtually shot out of the platform, a stream of dry sand flowed from the sand-pipes, smothering the slides of point-blades, bell-cranks and locking-bars, slots and tongues. The hands of the permanent-way staff were raised in angry protest, and the air was thick with their complaints, but Eldridge had gone. He was through Gas Works Tunnel and on towards Copenhagen before they realised that they were reviling the smoke which drifted slowly out and up from the tunnel mouth.

They said afterwards that there were clear traces of a tyre flange having ridden for five feet along the top of one of the check rails guarding the turn-out from No.11 Platform to the Down Main. Certainly the curve was never designed to carry such a speed. No-one had ever anticipated that such a speed would be reached in so short a distance. But if 2750 did ride up and mount the rail, she dropped back again instead of running over and off and so none on the train ever knew how close a thing it had been.

It was clear to both Inspector Bowles and Fireman

Clarke that Eldridge meant business right from the start. The former being unused to anything not strictly orthodox was already a little disturbed. The latter was much interested. Murmuring 'The old boy's in form today,' he bent briskly to his shovel in loyal support.

There was thus some spectacular running, with Wood

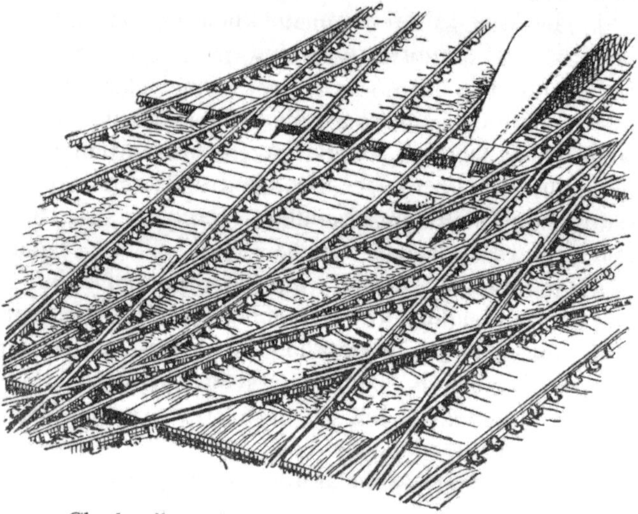

Check rails guarding the turn-out from platform 11

Green passed in 7 minutes 50 seconds at a speed of 70 mph exactly. At New Barnet this had risen to 72, and at Potter's Bar, top of the bank, to 75. Here Eldridge pulled up the gear to 30 per cent and without pretending to check, put the train through Hatfield Station at 94½ mph, sending Inspector Bowles reeling clean across the footplate.

'Here ! Steady, driver ! ' he bawled. 'Your

driving is reckless. If you aren't careful there'll be an accident.'

Eldridge pulled up the gear a little more. It was doubtful if he had even heard the official. He had no intention of heeding him for he knew now that he would break for the 100 mark down the next bank somewhere between Stevenage and Arlesey.

He beckoned Clarke over to him.

' I want the lot through Hitchin.'

' Right, mate ! '

At Woolmer Green Box, 23 miles 30 chains out, the train having taken 21 minutes 42 seconds and travelling at 85 mph, the needle began to climb. At Knebworth it was 89 ; at Stevenage 91 and then came the seven-mile gallop down the 1 in 200 bank.

With shrieking whistle 2750 flashed past Hitchin at 98, Bowles clinging terrified to the back of the fireman's seat, and Clarke, a little excited, firing furiously to hold the pressure. Only two more. Would she do it ?

Half way down ! But at Three Counties the needle touched the 100-mark, fell back to 99, then crossed to 102, the first time in the history of railways in Britain that a train had authentically travelled faster than a 100 mph !

' Ease her, I say, or I'll report you for reckless driving.'

But she needed no easing ; the hump beyond Arlesey brought the speed back into the 80's and, himself stirred, Eldridge was content to leave it there through Tempsford and St Neots.

Then came Offord ! Offord Curve, along the bank of the River Ouse, is super-elevated – i.e. banked up like a racing track – in a curve of 80 chains radius to allow trains to go round at a maximum speed of 70 mph. At this date it was without transitioning from the straight to the curves. Yet Eldridge, running at 88 mph within a mile of it, showed no sign that he intended to steady down.

' Offord, man ! Offord ! ' shrieked Bowles, now really frightened. ' Shut the regulator, man. We'll never get round ! '

The fear in his voice caused Clarke to look up. He had himself no doubt whether they would get round or not, although it did cross his mind that the old boy was certainly taking it pretty fast ; his concern was for the behaviour of this inspector chap, who seemed to be beside himself with fear. Pushing his shovel under the coal, Clarke stood beside him watching.

The regulator handle of the A3 class is duplicated on the fireman's side of the cab for convenience and so that it can be worked from either side. With scared eyes Inspector Bowles watched the free end before him until, unable to stand it any longer, his hand reached out and grasped it. In an instant the steam would have been shut off, but Clarke was quicker and struck his hand away.

' There's only one driver on this engine ! '

Too frightened to feel either anger or humiliation, Bowles's head turned to left and right when there came the warning from Eldridge, ' Hold tight ! ' and 2750 struck the curve at 86 mph.

She went round. Round the first curve. And then, with the hard thud of horn block crushing down onto axle-box as she heeled over, round the second reverse. But the group of gangers standing clear on the bank swore to a man afterwards that every inside wheel of the train was four inches clear of the rail as it passed.

At work in the end coach, observers and speed recorders with their squared paper and chronometers were flung from one side to the other as, indeed, they had been flung before that day, but this time with a sickening wait before the coach seemed to right itself. Through Hatfield and elsewhere they had been thrown across the floor, but almost immediately thrown back again ; this time it seemed that they were being pressed harder in a huddle against the panelling – and for a very long time.

But, though many broke under the load, the chairs held ; the train got round ; the coach righted ; Inspector Bowles resumed breathing ; Fireman Clarke resumed firing and Driver Eldridge the study of his cardboard schedule of timing.

2750 ran on, averaging a steady 86.

Stoke Bank reduced it to 81, but might not have been there for all the difference it made and then, just beyond Tuxford, came the first signal check, Markham ' Distant.'

Eldridge sounded the whistle, and the signal came off just as the train approached. But after he had cleared Gamston ' Home,' the signals for Retford Junction came into view, the whole lot set against him.

He whistled up again, but there was no response this time, and with a groan he shut the regulator and started to apply the brakes.

' That knocks the bottom out of any record time for King's Cross to Leeds,' he said. ' Don't know what's up, but whatever it is it's spoilt our run.'

Secretly well pleased with this unexpected turn of

events, Inspector Bowles began to solidify a little and to recover some of his self-assurance.

'Then you should know,' he said. 'We've overtaken the 10.5 out.'

Eldridge was astonished. But a quick calculation satisfied him that the inspector was right. Fast as was the timing of the 10.5, and notwithstanding its forty-five minute start, he had caught it up at Retford, a mere 138 miles out.

'Then we're done for!' he replied. 'They won't side-track it for us so near to Doncaster; we'll just have to amble along behind it till we take the Leeds Branch there.'

'It will do you no harm, my man, to steady yourself down a little. I feel it my bounden duty to enter in my report the manner in which you took the curve at Offord. Reckless in the extreme, most reckless, you will hear more about it!'

Since that little episode, Clarke had all but forgotten the presence of this singularly odious official. The words recalled it to him and with the need now only to play at firing for the rest of the run, his mischievously active brain began working.

The particular lump of coal that caught his eye was just the right shape, and just about the right weight if only he could get it in exactly the right place on the blade of his shovel.

His first attempt set it too central; he shook it off and fired normally; his second and third tries were also negative, but the fourth found the missile precisely where he wanted it; balanced to a quarter of an inch against the upturned, outer edge of the blade. During these malicious manoeuvres the rhythm of his firing was not affected by so much as a fraction of a second, it might have been a machine swinging the shovel to and fro in sweeping, graceful arcs, but as it swung this particular arc there was an imperceptible flick of the wrist and an eight-pound lump of coal terminated its parabolic path on the protruding ankle bone of the unsuspecting Headquarters Inspector Bowles.

'Sorry, Inspector. This old girl rides like a camel.'

With a howl of pain and a face of fury, Bowles jumped to his feet and, again almost as though he had anticipated something like this, Eldridge hastily called him over.

'Look here quickly, Inspector, this is more the sort of thing you need to report.'

Branching left and westward beyond Doncaster had brought a fairly stiff wind round to the right front corner which, combined with the high speed at which the engine was again travelling, created a low pressure area on the lee side, almost a partial vacuum, that sucked down into it the smoke and steam issuing from the chimney. Always when the speed approached 70 mph there was this drifting of smoke downward on the lee side, but when it approached 90, the drift became a definite smoke deflection, with the result, as now, that the weather-board look-out was completely obscured and, for all that could be seen from it, the train might as well have been running through a thick fog.

Inspector Bowles, torn between the desire to 'give this clumsy fireman a dressing down' and the need to give heed to the note of urgency in the driver's voice, postponed the former and limped scowling across the footplate to look out of the front window and see nothing but a blanket of swirling smoke and steam.

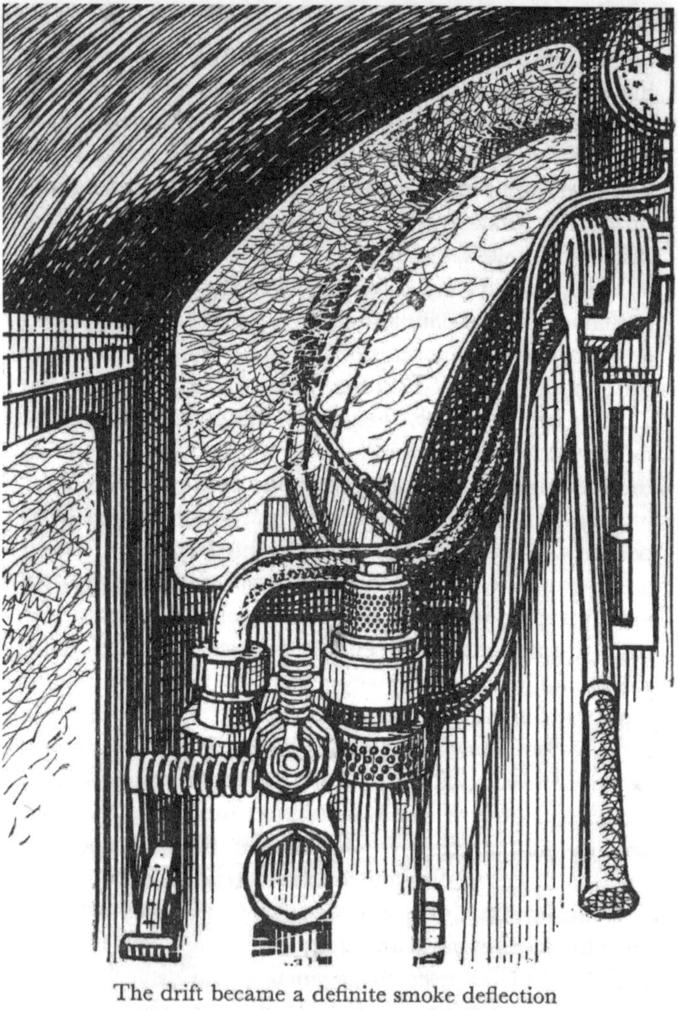

The drift became a definite smoke deflection

'Before you Headquarters people talk about running ninety-miles-an-hour trains regularly you'll have to think up something to overcome that little difficulty,' said Eldridge. 'I've been running more or less blind ever since we turned the corner, and I don't mind telling you now, I was running blind when we touched the hundred-mile figure. It isn't safe, and before we're asked to do it regularly you'll have to move the stuff out of the way and give us a clear look-out.'

So impressed was Inspector Bowles with the seriousness of what Eldridge was saying that Clarke, a little to his disappointment, was temporarily forgotten, though the effects of his skill were not, as was shown by the tender stroking of a bruised and swelling ankle.

But with only nine miles remaining, there was time neither for retribution nor for research into smoke deflection and as Eldridge eased the regulator all three men were prepared to make a truce while they had a brief rest and a meal. Then they started on the return run.

For it, Eldridge changed his tactics again, resolving to move smartly throughout, but to attempt one speed burst only – down the galloping ground of Stoke Bank.

He had been asked not only to touch the 100 mile-an-hour mark, which he had been able to do, but to 'hold it.' And this he felt he had not been able to do. The run up, therefore, though consistently fast, was less spectacularly so than the down had been, until on passing Grantham, Eldridge dropped the gear to 40 per cent, put a roaring exhaust through the chimney and achieved his intended flying start by running over the top of the bank at the even 75 mph.

Thereafter for the next ten minutes or so, excitement ran high in the third coach. There, in front of a large sheet of squared paper, sat the observation crew of four technicians : post caller, stop watch reader, equator, and recorder.

'Post ninety-six,' 'forty-four seconds,' 'eighty-one point eight miles per hour.'

'Post ninety-five,' 'forty-two seconds,' 'eighty-five point seven miles per hour.'

71 miles from London

A $\frac{3}{4}$ mile indicator

'Post ninety-four,' 'forty seconds,' 'ninety miles per hour.'

'Post ninety-three,' 'thirty-seven seconds,' 'ninety-seven point three miles per hour.'

'Post ninety-two,' 'thirty-five seconds,' 'one hundred and two point eight miles per hour.'

'Post ninety-one and a half,' 'seventeen seconds,' 'one hundred and five point nine miles per hour.'

'Post ninety-one,' 'sixteen point five seconds,' 'one hundred and nine point one miles per hour.'

'Post ninety and a half,' 'sixteen seconds,' 'one hundred and twelve point five miles per hour.'

'Post ninety,' 'sixteen seconds,' 'one hundred and twelve point five miles per hour.'

The voices of the tellers rose in their excitement as the points on the speed curve that was being plotted went higher and higher, until the curve reached its apex at 114.8 mph at Mile Post $87\frac{1}{4}$ – a speed unprecedented then, authoritatively or otherwise, in the annals of the railways !

On the engine there was now a different *feel*. 2750 no longer bumped up and down or from side to side. Under the feet of the men standing on it, the footplate became quite still. It was as though they were moving over ice or through air. The oscillations, both lateral and vertical, had been damped out. Smoke lay back viciously along the full length of the boiler barrel and completely obscured the look-out on the fireman's side, that of the driver being this time quite clear. Both the inspector and the fireman were doing their best to peer through the thick fog and help in sighting signals, but beyond an occasional glimpse, they could see very little. It was of no importance. Eldridge could read them and his speed indicator as well. Cool and steady, he divided his attention between the two, with yet another turn on the gear as he felt that the spent steam was getting clear of the cylinders without any check, in spite of the incredibly short time in which it had to be forced out. What an incomparable masterpiece was the design which enabled this to be done – the exhaust steam passages and the conjugate valve gear !

' Post eighty-six, eighteen seconds. The even one hundred miles per hour ! She has covered six and a quarter miles at an average of one hundred and eight point seven miles per hour ! Some driver ! '

Eldridge, in his quiet way, was pleased with the performance, too, but he took none of the credit to himself. He gave it all to the engine.

Others would one day run as fast and maybe faster, but somehow, in some way or other, always it was 2750 first. She led ; the field came after.

' A good fireman, my lad, takes an interest in the appearance of his footplate and keeps it spick and span. Just look at this front window, it's a disgrace, get a cloth and wipe it down.' It was the inspector again.

For a moment Clarke hesitated, and there was an ugly smouldering in his eyes, then suddenly his face cleared and, pulling his cap well down on his head, he took his cloth and started to make his way round the outside of the cab to the front of the window, which, it had to be confessed, was by now half blacked out with the sooted splashes from tunnel roofs.

Carefully, for although speed tests were now all over, the train was running in the high 60's near Huntingdon, he cleaned the front of the glass and returned to the cab to deal with the inside, supporting himself with outstretched left hand, thumb significantly near the catch.

Wiping with his right and watching in the glass the reflection of the approving inspector's face, he judged it to be in the right position for his purpose.

His thumb moved the fraction of an inch ; his head ducked ; the cab window flew open with a crash that nearly broke the glass ; a sixty-mile an hour gale of wind struck the inspector full in the face ; his well-brushed bowler hat lifted from his head ; it turned over twice as it soared gracefully back over the top of the tender, and then Clarke was prepared to call it a day.

Even Eldridge had been unprepared for this particular misadventure, and Clarke had to bear the full brunt of the inspector's wrath most of the remaining run to London. But with a clean engine-cloth tied like a scarf over his bald head, the inspector looked so like a Lancashire mill lass with trousers on, that there were compensations.

Watching him limp painfully off No.1 Arrival Platform, Eldridge looked severely across at his mate.

'As a top-link fireman, John Clarke, you ought to be thoroughly ashamed of yourself.'

Clarke grinned back happily, showing no sign of shame at all.

Chapter XI

COLLISION !

In the down road reception siding at Abbots Ripton, Driver Watson of New England Depot, his 39 trucks of mixed freight duly marshalled, decided to draw down to the outlet signal in readiness. He was working the afternoon pick-up goods to Peterborough with 4099, one of the older, wet steam, six-coupled J3 class freight types. He did not know that the guard, in less of a hurry, still had the brakes pinned down on a good half of the wagons, as well as the wheel hard round on those of his van. So when Watson opened the pilot valve of the old grid-iron type regulator valve on his engine it was not surprising that after the jangle of a few tightening three-link couplings it should jolt to a stop again.

Without pausing to consider what the cause might be, he took the line of laziness, and with the idea of giving the engine more steam, opened the regulator main valve to full port. Immediately there was a roar from the chimney which ejected what appeared to be a solid jet of black water ; the levels in the gauge glasses danced madly up and down, and the whole engine throbbed like a struck drum.

4099 had ' got hold of the water.'

This unhappy state results from any violent disturbance in the pressure of the steam at the top of the boiler or in the dome – such as happens, for instance, when the regulator valve is opened too fully and too quickly. The sudden rush of the steam through the throttle and down the pipes into the cylinders causes the pressure inside the dome to drop sharply. Other steam, with water mixed with it, rushes to this low pressure region and into the steam-pipes through the throttle. And before anything can be done *water itself* is passing through the steam-pipes, into the cylinders and out of the chimney just as though it were steam.

When priming reaches this state it becomes virtually impossible to move a regulator valve of the sliding surface type because the impact of the water on the face of the valve forces it hard up against the casting with a pressure that the operating mechanism has not been designed to overcome. The whole gear from handle to valve becomes as immovable as if its parts had been welded together.

Driver Watson made this disturbing discovery when he tried to remedy the results of his carelessness. With both hands on the top bend of the regulator handle and one foot on the bottom bend he exerted all his strength, but the lot was solid and he could tell by the feel of it that it could never be moved by him.

Alarmed, for the train was beginning to gather way, he called his fireman to his aid, only to find that the efforts of them both were equally in vain. There was only one thing to do ; bring the engine into mid-gear position which would cover the steam ports and stop the inrush of water.

But the reversing gear of the J3 class was worked by wheel, and to lift the links through half-travel took time. Frantically Watson pulled it round and round, for he found himself approaching the turn-out on to the down main.

As 2750 came over the brow of Stukeley Bank with the 5.30 p.m. Newcastle, the sharp eyes of Driver Eldridge saw the Reception Road outlet signal at danger ; that was in order. He also saw the train moving ; that, too, might be in order if the driver was drawing down to the signal ; he could not see at that distance in the darkness, yet there was something about the situation that he did not like. She seemed to be priming pretty badly, for instance. He touched the whistle and eased back the regulator. The sixth sense !

As he got nearer, his conviction grew that something was wrong. His speed was not high, as they had only just topped Stukeley, but he destroyed five inches of vacuum and brought it lower. Clarke looked up on feeling this unusual check and went to his look-out expecting to see a signal ' ON.'

Instead he saw the freight engine still throwing out volumes of water from the chimney and very near now to the fouling point.

His Mutual Improvement Class instruction told him exactly what was occurring, and he knew, perhaps better than his driver, what the result would be.

' He's *got hold of the water*, and can't shut the regulator ! '

There had been no Mutual Improvement Classes when Eldridge was a cleaner, and he might have found it difficult to connect this cause and effect, but the school of experience can teach its lessons too. Albeit through different channels, both men knew the same thing. That train would come out on to the main line against the signal.

Full on went the brakes and the whistle shrilled.

Would they stop clear ?

The J3 ' takes hold of the water '

The speed was down to 18 mph when Eldridge decided that they would not, for the buffer beam of 4099 was already in his path.

' We shall hit her ! Hold tight ! '

Clarke needed no warning. Bracing himself against the scoop pillar behind his mate he waited calmly for the impending collision.

It came with a grinding metallic clang as the left outside cylinder of 2750 caught the right-hand leading wheel of the J3. There was a violent jerk sideways on the footplate, a pause, and then a surge forward again. The right-hand side of 4099 lifted slowly, her three coupled wheels hanging ridiculously in the air, then, as gently as if being put to bed, she rolled over on to her side.

2750 jolted forward thirty yards, pushed on by the weight of the train, before coming to a stand with all wheels (both of engine and tender) off the rails and foul of the up main line.

The immediate movements of Fireman Clarke in the quietness that followed would have gladdened the eyes of his chief, who spared no effort in training his staff to deal with every emergency.

Without waiting for any instruction from his driver he stepped quickly across the footplate to the tool cupboard, and from the metal cylinder containing them slipped half a dozen detonators into his pocket. Then, taking a red flag, he got down from the footplate ; crossed over to up main four foot way and, with elbows well in, set off at a brisk trot in the down direction.

Listening as he ran and watching the up road signals, he continued until he estimated he had gone about a quarter of a mile, then stooped to clip a detonator on the rail. At another quarter of a mile, another detonator, and at the third quarter mile three detonators three paces apart. Then, with his red flag spread he sat down on the bank to recover his breath and light a cigarette, ready as soon as he heard it to stop the first up train to appear.

Back at the scene of the collision, Driver Eldridge, having assured himself that neither of the enginemen on 4099 had suffered more than a shaking, advised throwing out the fire in case the top corner of the firebox should be uncovered and then went forward, ruefully to examine the damage done to his engine. He found the left corner of the buffer beam turned back almost to a right angle, the outside gusset stay-plate virtually flattened and the leading end of the footplate bent into an arch. Worse was the damage to the left cylinder, the cover of which was smashed to pieces, exposing the front side of the piston head and an ugly score along the cylinder wall. Both cylinder cocks had been ripped off and the 'motion,' too, had suffered as 2750 had scraped by before the other turned over clear. The combination and union links were both buckled and although he could not see it, Eldridge had little doubt but that the valve spindle would have been bent as well. The engine was a complete casualty and would not be able to work home under her own steam. Realising this, he went back gloomily to the footplate to await the return of his fireman.

Meantime, at the other end of the train, the guard had been protecting its rear in a manner similar to, though considerably slower than, that of Clarke. And this done, he continued still farther to the nearest signal-box to tell the signalman what had occurred and to pilot back the assisting engine that would come down from Hitchin to draw off the coaches and set them in a siding.

Thus was started once again the ringing of bells and the tapping of morse keys.

‘ Abbots Ripton South Box, that Control ? I'm reporting both main lines blocked at the outlet from the down reception siding. Pick-up goods came out against the signal and was hit by the engine of the five-thirty p.m. Newcastle. Nobody hurt. Goods blocking both roads. Detonators placed for both directions.’

And Control to Depot :

‘ Send breakdown vans to Abbot's Ripton, both main lines blocked, complete stoppage. Pacific off down main all wheels engine and tender, J class engine turned over. Path ready for train in fourteen minutes.’

And depot foreman to superintendent, just drawing chair to table for his evening meal :

‘ Both roads blocked at Abbots Ripton, sir. The vans will leave in twenty minutes.’

Twenty minutes filled with haste and activity, but ordered activity ; nowhere even a semblance of bustle or confusion ; the functioning of an organisation that it had taken years of careful study and patient training to build up.

To each of three lads were handed four wooden strips bearing the painted names and addresses of those of the breakdown gang who lived within the ‘ Calling Up ’ area of the particular call boy. Mounted on cycles always kept in first class condition by the depot fitters they were off and away at once, calling out the most distant man last, and leaving the cycle for his use.

' Take Seventeen-Forty-two off the eight-forty for the vans, Jim. I'll find something else to cover it before then.'

A simple enough instruction, but one which displayed a wealth of sound judgement and decision, for 1742, one of the J20 class 0-6-0 freight types, had a 4 feet 8 inch coupled wheel, large enough to get the train along at a good speed and not be too long on the way, yet small enough to make the engine suitable for any heavy chain pulling work that might be required when it arrived. The enginemen, too, were of just the right type for what might prove to be a big breakdown job ; quick to respond to an order, however out of the usual it might be, but neither reckless nor careless ; able to give a strong, steady pull when asked for and not the snatch that so often spelt a broken chain.

Jim himself pilots the engine through the depot and couples it to the vans, now brightly lit up. For the first of the gang has appeared and, having unlocked doors and cupboards, is busy lighting the fires, for this sounds like an all night job, and the early mornings of January are cold.

In ones and twos the remainder of the gang join him, the driver of the big 35-ton breakdown crane going directly to his little cabin high up on the slewing platform, to coax the fire into giving him a full head of steam well before it will be needed ; the hydraulic jack operators charging and testing their jacks ; the van-steward supplementing his food stores with new bread and such other victuals as he has been able to commandeer at short notice from canteen and refreshment room ; the foreman of the breakdown gang overseeing the operations of all and checking the arrivals of his men ; ordered movement the keynote throughout.

Last appears the superintendent, not in the best of moods, with a carefully prepared meal left untasted. He looks over the men ; approves the measures taken to power the train ; has a word or two with the foreman and the guard ; and climbs up to the special compartment of the riding van set aside for his use, there to be a little mollified by the appearance in less than two minutes of a smart van-steward with a plate of freshly cut sandwiches, another of dry biscuits and a pot of steaming hot coffee.

The ‘ Right ’ signal is given ; the train is away and as she carries express passenger headlights, is soon travelling at speed towards the scene of the blockage. At Hatfield the superintendent calls in his foreman and together they discuss the probabilities of the situation and, from the little information as yet received, plan the best line of action.

At Abbots Ripton down home she is checked and slows to a stop, drawing forward again with caution up to the obstruction. Here the two men get down onto the ballast, and with their powerful acetylene hand lamps examine at close quarters the size of the job and the ‘ lie ’ of the two engines. While they are so engaged others of the gang are lighting up the scene with vapour oil lamps and acetylene flares, getting out jacks and packing from the tool and packing vans and such other tackle as they know will be required. The job surveyed, the superintendent confers with his colleagues from the traffic and engineer’s departments, who are also present, and the big crane is brought forward, jib slowly rising and ' bull's horn ' hook carrying two 20 ton chains. Thereafter the superintendent's becomes a watching brief, but with the weight of much experience, a very valuable watching brief. If a jack or wedge is so placed as to endanger any of the gang his keen eye will see it and a momentary halt be called ; if the angle of the crane jib or the position of the load on the hook makes a lift liable to overturn the crane he will know and every man in the gang is aware that he is watching their safety and works the better for the knowledge.

But actual operations are controlled now and instructions given by the breakdown foreman, his voice clear and decisive.

' Cut here and here ! ' He points to the wrist-thick drawbar between engine and tender, safety bars as well. And his words are quickly followed by the hiss of the burner and a stream of sparks which light up the masked, leather-gauntletted, oxy-acetylene operator whose tiny blue flame cuts through the metal as easily as a knife through cheese.

Engine and tender separated, round swings the crane jib, and the foreman, through his ' mouthpiece ' standing on the platform, controls its movements.

' Take the weight steady ! ' ' Lift a little ! ' ' Raise jib ! ' ' Lift again ! ' ' Lower the rope ! ' ' Slew left ! ' ' Lower the rope ! ' ' Little right ! ' ' Lower off ! ' and the trailing tender wheels are back on the road.

Steadily the crane ' paddles ' forward ; the hooks are placed round the front beam. The operations are gone through again and the leading wheels also drop back on to the road.

' Pinch her off ! '

Six men, three on each side, with long pinch bars inserted between tyre and rail, inch the tender back away from the engine, leaving elbow room for dealing with this tougher proposition. It is easy enough to lift with so powerful a crane, but hard to slew with the trailing pony wheels deep-bedded in the soft ballast, and the leading end must go on first.

Well, plenty of light is the most urgent necessity. Flares and lamps are concentrated. Next the crane is shored up and stiffened for very nearly her maximum load. Both girders are drawn out now and packed up from the sleepers ; two hydraulic jacks as well, between the underframe and the other sleepers. The tail weight is set right back to give the maximum cantileverage possible and a special examination made of the dog-clips securing the end frame girders to the rails.

So far, so good ! She won't tip sideways. But what about endways, with the tail weight set so far back ? A watch is kept for this possibility, and the jib put well down to offset it until some load can be put on to the hook.

The chains come slowly down. Their great hooks, well spread, are set under the buffer beam and the deep-toned order of the foreman booms : ' Take the weight steady.'

They tauten and balance the load of the tail weight.

' Jib up ! ' is the next order, and it must be right up, almost to the vertical, for the load must come on to the crane with the least possible overturning moment.

' Hold that ! ' And there is a short pause while a final survey is made. The hooks are well home, crane girders well braced, track standing up, jib set and stable.

'Take her up!' comes the order. And the gang stands back clear, watchful for any unforeseen contingency, alert and competent.

The sound of the crane now changes from the noisy roar of a few minutes ago to a low, almost quiet hum as the enormous load comes fairly on the chains, the strain on the teeth of the gears stops the vibration and rattle ; now and again there is a loud crack as a dog clip or shackle shifts position and snaps home to a surer seating. There is the protesting creak from compressed wood packing under jacks and girders, but by degrees, almost imperceptibly, the leading end of 2750, her heavy cylinders, valve gear, bogie, coupled wheels and boiler, rises inch by inch.

'Hold that!' She is high enough to bring the trailing coupled clear of the rail top and permit the slew ; but not a quarter of an inch higher than necessary.

'Slew right.' The hum re-starts and the crane hook moves right. The leading end of the engine follows after a pause. The hook moves right again. The front end follows again, but this time in a lurch that ends in an abrupt and sullen stop. The trailing pony wheels, about which the engine must be swung round, are deeply embedded, and will not let the front end go any further.

No use trying to shift her with the crane, the jib is too near the vertical to permit a pull sideways ; to pursue that line will be to bring the steel rope out of its groove in the jib pulley and perhaps break it too and drop the load with a crash.

'Two ten-tonners here!' 'Here' are the tyres of the right-hand bogie wheels for the jack heads, and the adjacent rail for the feet. Each operator wedges the head of his jack and pumps until the front end gives a further lurch and brings the crane rope more nearly to the vertical.

'Try her right again.' This time there is a full fifteen tons behind the sideways pull of the rope and in long jerks, but irresistibly, the front end swings round until the flanges of the bogie wheels are directly over the rails.

'Lower steady!' They gradually approach each other. 'Lower off!' and the leading end is re-railed.

The trailing end, though heavy, is easier to handle, for now there is a free pivot about which to slew it when lifted. The crane is released, moved forward, and re-secured. The cab roof is taken off and the chains passed through and hooked under the drag-box casting. They lift, slew, lower, and the engine is on.

'Square her!' And the jib is brought square with the jib truck and lowered onto its riding cradle. Engine and tender are chain coupled and after a close examination to make quite sure that both are fit to travel, they are attached to the engine sent down for the purpose and towed carefully, temporarily crippled giants, back to their home depot for the stripping of damaged parts and their repair.

Smedley replaces his watch. It is two hours eight minutes from the time of arrival to clearing both main lines. But for the bogging of the trailing pony wheels it would have been under the hour and three-quarters. Nice work! Well satisfied, he signals the break-down gang into the riding-van for a rest before tackling the overturned engine, thrown well clear of the down main. Gangers of the Engineer's Department, the site cleared, are busy replacing broken chairs and re-aligning the track.

In the van the superintendent joins his men and like them buries his teeth into ham and corned beef sandwiches, each a good two inches thick. He drinks steaming hot tea from a pint mug ungraced by such needless embellishment as handle or saucer, and for twenty minutes he rests with them. Then he rises with a ‘ More to be done, men ! ’ and the gang follow him, refreshed and ready.

Though looking by far the more difficult part of the night's work, actually the righting of the six-coupled J3 is a much easier proposition than re-railing the Pacific because of the former's lighter weight.

Lights and flares are re-concentrated ; the crane is re-set ; and spades are brought out to dig channels under the engine so that the big lifting chains may be passed right underneath the engine and the hooks anchored low down on the under side.

Engine and tender are separated as before by flame cutting through the drawbar and when the latter has been re-railed and pinched back clear, the chains are positioned, great care is taken to see that they will not foul or tie up as the engine rights.

Slowly the load is put on to them, and again the well-trained gang stand back clear, as, tautening, there is the inevitable crack of slipped packings as they shift and settle home. ‘ Hold that ! ’ comes this time when the engine has been tilted a foot or so and the foreman is satisfied that he has got a sound hold on it. The gang close in again and stack up baulks of timber to fend the high side wheels when they drop, then clear again as his voice calls out the order ‘ Take her up steady.’

Inch by inch, but inexorably, the engine rights. The

craneman, himself an expert, judging the moment when the centre of gravity will enter the middle third. The instant it does so, he changes lift to lower, and the hook falls rapidly as the engine falters a moment and then, with a thump, drops back on to her wheels.

Thereafter the work is straightforward ; hooks are shifted to the front buffer beam and then, the leading wheels on, to the cab end. ' Take the weight steady ! ' ' Take her up ! ' ' Slew left ! ' ' Lower steady ! ' ' Left again ! ' ' Lower off ! '

There follows a brief interval of silence in which backs are straightened, tired muscles flexed, cigarettes lit in an atmosphere of ' So much for that ! ' Then the bustle of packing up begins.

The crane jib is squared and lowered, hook neatly housed in its cradle, chains coiled up in their lockers ; the fire damped down ; jacks, packing and gear thrown anyhow into the appropriate van, to be sorted, cleaned, sharpened and stowed properly next day. Lights are collected and doused ; wearied but satisfied men climb up to their seats. The superintendent has a final word with traffic officers about disposal of the damaged engine ; headlights are changed from express passenger to stopping passenger positions, and the breakdown train rumbles off towards the shed and the homes of the men. Given luck in the run and not too much side-tracking, there may yet be time for an hour or two in bed.

Or will there instead be a spread of wagons at Hitchin and another knock on the door just as the warmth of blankets is beginning to seep through to chilled bones ?

There probably will !

CHAPTER XII

THE GREEN ENGINE IS NOT RUNG OUT

Yet another winter's running had come to an end when one Tuesday evening in early April Eldridge was sent for by his chief. He felt a certain uneasiness, perhaps because he had been told to report when he had finished his turn of duty instead of when signing on. As he got near the office his uneasiness deepened to apprehension.

It had long been the custom, when there was ill news or blame to hand out to an engineman, to keep it until he came in from his day's work. The unwritten law, rigidly kept, was that the management should not do anything to worry or distract an engine-crew going out on the road. So if an engineman was sent for when he came off duty he expected trouble.

As he entered the office, therefore, and confronted his chief and Inspector Talbot, Eldridge did not show the brisk self-confidence he usually did in the presence of his superiors. Nor did the kindly 'Afternoon, Eldridge' with which he was greeted altogether reassure him. For spread out on the table were very many Drivers' Repair Sheets, and he recognised the handwriting on them as his own. They were the sheets of 2750.

Smedley, who knew his men down to the working of their minds, saw the putting of two and two together which was going on in Eldridge's head. He pulled a wry face.

'Coming in long and frequently, Eldridge!'

'Yes, sir, I've had to book a few things recently.'

'The most serious is "Off steam." It appears on every one of these sheets, and the foreman fitter is worried a bit. He has a reputation as well as you, you know, and brought them to me with his opinion of the cause.'

'It's a job sometimes to hold her over, but no doubt it's the coal. We've had some poor stuff lately ; when it isn't dust it's iron.'

Smedley looked up at him with a smile.

'Our main line bunkers are never charged but with best Yorkshire hards, Eldridge. It isn't coal, my friend, as I suspect you know. It's miles. Twenty-seven-Fifty has run a total of more than a hundred and thirty thousand, a magnificent performance that reflects the highest credit on you as her driver. You must have handled her well to have got that mileage on first-grade express work ; but it is beginning to tell now.'

He passed his hand across the sheets before him.

'"Off steam." Why ? Because of leaks past the pistons. We've re-sleeved and re-ringed the valves and would again, but we can't re-sleeve the cylinders. They're worn oversize, they're three thirty-secondths oval in places ; they can't hold back the steam from leaking past.

'"Off steam." Because every pin in the motion is worn and slack. Maybe not more than a sixty-fourth, but multiply that by the number of pins and you'll understand why we cannot any longer set your valves to the knife edge accuracy that has always been the secret of your success with this engine.

'Then there's your tyres, worn down to scrapping size and some of the tender plates are through to paper thickness, too.'

‘ I pass over the effect of those miles in ways that may be less apparent to you, boiler stays short and a thin area on the left side of the wrapper plate, scaled tubes and many other things I could mention. I'm afraid it's no use, Eldridge. Twenty-seven-Fifty is due for a general repair in main works and a path has been arranged for her on Thursday. You have run her long and run her well and I appreciate your work ; it is such consistently high performance as yours that has earned us our good name.’

Eldridge accepted what he had known all along to be the inevitable.

‘ Very good, sir. I hope she will be my engine again when she comes back, I should feel odd now on any other ! ’

Smedley glanced across at his inspector before he replied.

‘ Unfortunately, Eldridge, she won't be coming back. That really is the reason why I wanted to see you this afternoon. We thought, Inspector Talbot and I, that some explanation was due to you because, like everybody else at this depot, we know how much this particular engine means to you.

In a way, by an ironic twist of fate, you are yourself responsible for her transfer away from us, since it is the direct result of that fine success of yours that November with the high speed trials between London and Leeds. Because of that success it has been decided that high-speed running on our main line routes is a practicable and, we hope, a paying proposition and several units are to be introduced within the next few weeks or so.

You may remember that I mentioned at the time that a new type of locomotive might have to be built, especially to work these super-fast trains. That has proved to be the case.

The new engine is a development of the A3 class, but thirty pounds higher pressed and with slightly smaller cylinders. There are one or two other differences as well. External appearance for one. What I suggested might happen has happened. These A4 class engines are streamlined, partly to reduce the head-on wind resistance, but principally, you'll be interested to learn, because of the difficulty you experienced on the trial runs with smoke drifting along the boiler barrel and obscuring the look-out.

They scratched their heads a lot about that ; did tests in wind tunnels – the ones they use for aeroplanes, you know. Tried all kinds of shapes for a front end that would send the smoke clear. They've finished up with what they call the " Horizontal Wedge." And it's thanks entirely to your report on the trial run.

I'm telling you all this, Eldridge, to soften the blow a little for you, for we have been selected for the job of working these trains. And the new engines will come here for the job. The A3 class, with yours among them, are being withdrawn from the depot and will be transferred to the Northern districts.

The first of the batch will be worked up from the plant on Thursday, and the men will take back 2750. I'm sorry, but we cannot, and must not, want to hold up the progressive ideas of our superiors. What we have to do is to help them with our loyal cooperation. If it is any consolation to you, you will take over the new arrival and have the satisfaction of working the first of the " Flyers ".'

There was little enthusiasm in Eldridge's reply.

'Thank you, sir, and I appreciate it that you should put me on the first trip. There'll be a lot outside who will envy that, but all the same I can't help saying that I'd rather have Twenty-seven-Fifty on a "Parly".'

'That's natural enough the way you feel at the moment, but you'll see the matter differently a little later on and, anyway, you know, it doesn't follow that Twenty-seven-Fifty when she comes out of Plant will be the same that went in.'

'You mean she may not be so good? I know from my own experience that that often happens. Why does it, sir?'

'That's a question I've often asked myself, Eldridge. And a good many others of us have asked it too. But we've never been able to find a really satisfactory explanation. You may have two engines not only of identical design from the same works, but even built by the same men on the same pit. Yet one will steam and pull, and the other sulk and slack.

Take Twenty-seven-Forty-six, for instance, an engine that nobody will take if they can help it, and she's guaranteed to lose time if they do. Yet she's one of the same batch as Twenty-seven-Fifty – only four before her as a matter fact. And they were turned out within a month of each other.'

'There must be a reason!' broke in Talbot.

'Probably a combination of many. A knowing old charge-hand spotting a porous casting or an over-hardened pin, and shying away from it, leaving it for the raw hand – I saw one once with his bare arm buried in the port ways of a cylinder casting feeling for lumps and sand-holes ! That sort of thing makes a difference. But not all the difference. And it's hard to account for the rest – very hard.

'Let's hope, Eldridge, that your new streamlined job, the battleship-grey flyer, will have been built that way, and that you'll make her as famous as you have made Twenty-seven-Fifty.'

'Thank you, sir, but I doubt it. I'll do my best with her. And I hope I'll turn out some good work. But there's never before been an engine like Twenty-seven-Fifty, and I think there never will be again.'

'He's right there,' added Inspector Talbot.

'Well, well, we shall see, Eldridge. Take a look round the newcomer when she gets in on Thursday, and try her out on the ten-fifty on Friday.'

With this the interview closed and Eldridge in a very mixed frame of mind walked slowly through the yard and home to his tea.

Nor was there the usual cheerfulness in his greeting to his mates as in twos and threes he passed them on the way back again two days later to sign on for the 4.15 with engine No.4472. His own engine was in steam in No.4 Road. The men who had brought up the first of the fleet of streamliners were going to take her back.

More than one eyed him sympathetically, but a good many of the younger men looked at him with envy, for the news had got round, and a good deal of interest had been aroused throughout the depot. He went straight to '72, passing both his own engine and the hump-backed, flat-snouted, dull grey monster that stood in No.8 Road, the centre of an admiring group of enginemen and mechanics alike.

The newcomer

Among these was Fireman Clarke, a little arrogant and self-important, but more interested in his plans to get 2750, the green engine, well and truly ' rung out ' when she left, than in the imposing, if inartistic, lines of the grey 2509.

' Ringing out ' is an ear-splitting, nerve-racking device of the devil used by young and light-hearted artisans wherever there are workshops, spanners and iron plate, to express communal approval, disapproval, celebration, condemnation and anything else that can serve as excuse for creating an infernal thunder.

Originally of the works machine-shop, it consists of the rhythmic beating of spanner or hammer on the sheet iron guard of gear wheels. With forty or so performers, in the enclosed space of such a shop, it can be impressive. When the number approaches a hundred and forty the noise is quite unforgettable.

Clarke had joyfully roped in most of the staff of the depot into his army of ringers, and they were ready when he gave the signal to say goodbye to 2750 in a way really worthy of a locomotive so distinguished and a driver so popular. They would use footplates and splashers for gear-guards, and Clarke was counting on a really good five minutes of pandemonium.

But there was work to be done first, and having run his eye over the cab fittings of the new arrival, judged pretty accurately the heat that would be trapped by the rubber roofing between engine and tender, tested the comfort of his bucket seat and given the onlookers his not too flattering opinion of the complete unit, he went to join his mate in the preparation of 4472 standing on the pit outside No.2 Road.

And while they were so employed, 2750 passed them on No.4 on her way to the water crane to top up before leaving. Her ‘ foreign ’ crew, were completely unaware that they were taking something more than an engine from the man they passed. He did not pause in his task of charging the side-rod oil wells of 4472. He did not even lift his head.

The crane bag was dropped from the filling hole and fell with the splash of its emptying water. The fireman clambered forward over the coal to his place on the footplate and the driver appeared at the cab side awaiting the ‘ Right ’ signal from the running foreman.

Clarke decided this was the moment for ‘ Action Stations.’ Moving carefully so as not to be seen by his mate, he slipped out from the pit and armed himself with a large and vicious-looking inch double-ended spanner. The others followed him with their eyes, waiting for the signal.

The foreman gave the order ‘ Right, mate, drop down.’ The regulator opened. Steam roared out below from the cylinder cocks. The rods clanked as she slipped a half turn, and then the engine moved slowly down towards the outlet.

Still, Eldridge went on quietly with his oiling and still he did not lift his head, two things which woke the understanding of Fireman Clarke to a little of what he must be feeling. For a moment he hesitated, looking hard at the older man, then he knew what to do. Putting the spanner carefully down on the ground he turned to those others, waved his hand to and fro across his face and shook his head. Something in the attitude of Eldridge wasn’t according to plan. Clarke could not have explained why, but he knew instinctively that this was not the moment for noise. He just stood quietly and watched him.

And as the tail lamps of the engine passed round the curve towards the tunnel mouth, her old driver did look up. He did not in the end deny himself a last glimpse of the apple-green engine, so massive and yet, somehow, slender and sleek, like a thoroughbred.

Watching her go, thinking of the times he had had with her, good and bad ; remembering the hard pull up Stoke Bank with the double train ; and the time when they hit the 100-mark, and held it ; and getting stuck in the tunnel ; and hauling the *Flying Scotsman* ; and running in through Hatfield in the early mornings with the sun rising – he nodded his head.

With 2750 he had got a deeper satisfaction than out of anything else in his life. It made him happy now just to think of some of the runs he had had with her. He would never forget them.

But he could not help shaking his old head at the thought that his days of pioneering and record-breaking were over. He would no longer be the first to do this, first to pass that. From now on he would be just one of the field.

2750 had gone.